SO-BEZ-353

ALSO AVAILABLE FROM
LAUREL-LEAF BOOKS

ALSO BY SHERRI L. SMITH

Lucy the Giant

Sparrow

SHERRI L. SMITH

Hot, Sour, Salty, Sweet

This is a work of fiction. Names, characters, places, and incidents either are the product of the author's imagination or are used fictitiously. Any resemblance to actual persons, living or dead, events, or locales is entirely coincidental.

Copyright © 2008 by Sherri L. Smith

All rights reserved. Published in the United States by Laurel-Leaf, an imprint of Random House Children's Books, a division of Random House, Inc., New York. Originally published in hardcover in the United States by Delacorte Press, New York, in 2008.

Laurel-Leaf Books with the colophon is a registered trademark of Random House, Inc.

Visit us on the Web! www.randomhouse.com/teens

Educators and librarians, for a variety of teaching tools, visit us at www.randomhouse.com/teachers

The Library of Congress has cataloged the hardcover edition of this work as follows:

Smith, Sherri L.
Hot, sour, salty, sweet / Sherri L. Smith.
p. cm.
Summary: Disaster strikes when Ana Shen is about to deliver the salutatorian speech at her junior high school graduation, but an even greater crisis looms when her best friend invites a crowd to Ana's house for dinner, and Ana's multicultural grandparents must find a way to share a kitchen.
ISBN 978-0-385-73417-2 (trade)—ISBN 978-0-385-90431-5 (glb)—ISBN 978-0-375-84639-7 (e-book)
[1. Interpersonal relations—Fiction. 2. Family life—California—Los Angeles—Fiction. 3. Cookery—Fiction. 4. Graduation (School)—Fiction. 5. Parties—Fiction. 6. Racially mixed people—Fiction. 7. Los Angeles (Calif.)—Fiction.] I. Title.
PZ7.S65932Hot 2008
[Fic]—dc22
2007015035

ISBN 978-0-440-23988-8 (pbk.)

RL: 5.1
Printed in the United States of America
10 9 8 7 6 5 4 3 2

First Laurel-Leaf Edition

For my family—past, present and future

ACKNOWLEDGMENTS

Special thanks to J.H. for trying to fix my Mandarin, and to K.M. for his childhood memories and cultural insights. Any errors that slipped by them are 100% mine!

1

Here's how she wants it to go: After the graduation ceremony, when all the speeches are done, Jamie Tabata will walk off the stage with her, take her by the hand and say, "Ana Shen, would you please go to the dance with me tonight?"

Ana, of course, will say yes. She might even blush and squeeze his hand a little. And then she will go home, ignore her family for the next four hours and spend the fifth hour getting dressed (maybe the blue skirt and the pale blue tank top with the ruffles) and taming her hair. When Jamie shows up, they'll walk to the school together, even though it's a long walk. The gym will be lit up like the Fourth of July, with a mirror ball casting starlight and shadows so that even the bleachers look otherworldly. And their first dance will be a slow dance (but not too slow) and he will pull her close and say, "I've liked you since the first day I saw you."

Ana will say, "Me too." And the dance will end, but they will still both be standing there, his arms around her, and he will lean in and give her the most perfect—

"Now, our salutatorian, Ana Shen!" Principal Rubens bellows into the microphone. The mike squeals and Ana jumps out of her reverie.

Great, Ana. Daydreaming right in the middle of your own graduation. She's on her feet before she knows it. Jamie Tabata is making his way back to his seat. Valedictorian, first in their class. He smiles shyly at Ana. She's too embarrassed to smile back. She blushes. Ana's had a big old crush on Jamie since the second grade, and today is the last day of junior high school. She may never see him again after this. And "this" is a perfect chance to make a fool out of herself by flubbing her graduation speech.

She grins a bit too widely at Principal Rubens, an avocado-shaped man in a brown suit with a fringe of hair and beard to match. He holds his hand out to offer her the podium. Ana takes a deep breath and tries to focus.

The sun is out. It is a beautiful June day in Los Angeles. The soft whir of the freeway sounds like the earth breathing, like bees humming in a meadow. The sky is blue, sprinkled with airplanes like distant birds. The stage is set up at one end of the school's sports field, row upon row of plastic folding chairs before her, filled with purple graduation gowns and parents in business suits and Sunday dresses. Her family is somewhere in the crowd—parents, little brother, both sets of grandparents. *Come on, Ana,* she tells herself. *Don't barf. Just do your speech.*

She steps up to the mike and clears her throat.

"Good afternoon, soon-to-be graduates of Edison Junior High. My name is Ana Shen."

The crowd rumbles. Ana hesitates, to let the applause die down. It does, but the rumbling does not.

She begins again. "When we first started at Edison . . ." The rumbling is louder, louder than the freeway behind them. Louder than the crowd. She looks uncertainly at Principal Rubens.

"Is that an earthquake?" someone asks.

There is a sudden hush. And then, behind her, the roof of the gymnasium explodes. Or, rather, a geyser of water blows through the roof, shooting into the air like Old Faithful, three stories high. It arcs over the stage with a rainbow dazzle of water and sprays the back half of the sports field like a giant sprinkler. Ana ducks behind the podium as the water shoots overhead. People sitting in the back rows scream. The stream of water loses pressure and falls, like heavy rain, onto the graduates and their families. The purple dye in the gowns starts to run, and the graduates caught in the deluge do a little dance, yanking off their gowns and running past the edge of the falling water.

Oh no, thinks Ana. *My hair.*

It's not the kind of hair that stands up well to water. Ana clutches her graduation cap to her head. Principal Rubens jumps to his feet, pushing Ana to the side.

"Remain calm, everyone! Remain calm! We appear to have broken a pipe somewhere! Remain calm!"

No one remains calm, however. Teachers go scampering off the stage, and a few chairs are overturned as families plunge through the forming mud, looking for shelter and drier ground. "Head for the far end of the field!" Principal Rubens shouts into the microphone. It squeals again, and the sound works as an alarm. The teachers suddenly remember themselves and organize Ana's classmates into groups that can actually follow orders.

So much for how she wanted it to go. Ana climbs off the wet stage alone, her mortarboard dripping with purple water. Oddly, the rest of her is relatively dry. She doesn't even want to think about what her hair looks like. In the chaos, she spots Chelsea. They grab hands, find a relatively dry spot beneath a jacaranda tree and wait for an official announcement.

"Here." Chelsea offers Ana a dry graduation program.

"Thanks." Ana takes off her cap and shakes her hair out. She dries her face with the program, dissolving the proud letters declaring EDISON JUNIOR HIGH COMMENCEMENT CEREMONIES.

Not the way Ana planned it at all.

"We should find our families," she says at last.

"Ah, they'll be fine," Chelsea replies. "Besides, look at this mess. They could be anywhere."

It's true. Ana surveys the devastation. It looks like Noah's flood has hit the sports field. Water is running toward the softball diamond, pooling at home plate and third. More of the students are pulling off their gowns. A few of them are laughing. Mostly the boys. The girls look mortified.

"Geez," Ana says. "These gowns stain. I can't believe they made us buy them." She looks down. Hers is dry. Everything but her head and shoes.

"What?" Chelsea shimmies out of her gown, smoothing out her sky blue sundress as she goes. "Told you they were too cheap to be good. This stuff'll never wash out."

"You're not even wet," Ana says.

Chelsea shrugs. "I'm lucky. I can dodge raindrops."

Ana grins. "Right. And I can block them with my head."

"So . . . any sign of Jamie?"

Ana looks around and sighs. "Nope. And it's probably for the best. I don't exactly look fetching right now, do I?"

She squeezes her hair and a stream of water runs out. She sighs again. At least she can give herself a makeover before tonight. Being asked *to* dance is almost as good as being asked to *go to* the dance. "Help me braid it back?"

Chelsea smoothes her own straight sandy-brown hair. "What are friends for?"

Ana braids one side, Chelsea the other, while they

5

wait for the principal to return. Ten minutes later, Ana looks less of a wreck, and Principal Rubens has taken the stage again.

"Ladies and gentlemen, I apologize. We've been experiencing plumbing difficulties over the last week," the principal announces over the squawking microphone.

Chelsea whispers to Ana, "Yeah, I heard the sixth graders flushed bananas down all the toilets on the second floor."

"Gross."

Principal Rubens pauses and rubs a handkerchief over his bald spot. He wipes his eyes and stuffs it back into his jacket.

"It appears that the water main has in fact burst—" Someone squeals. "*Not* the sewer main, as some of the young men here have suggested." He gives a stern look at the group the squeal came from. "But, in fact, the water main has broken and flooded"—he actually sobs here and catches himself—"flooded the gymnasium. The beautiful wood floors are ruined. The expense. I—" He stops again and pulls out the handkerchief to mop his face. "I'm sorry to say, the graduation dance will have to be canceled. I repeat, there will be no dance tonight. Sorry, boys and girls. I truly am."

"Oh, Ana," Chelsea says, and puts a hand on her arm.

Ana's jaw drops. A split second later, one of her braids sproings apart and unworks itself into a frizzy bush. Principal Rubens goes on about how the ceremony will continue at the far end of the field—no more speeches, just handing out the diplomas so everyone can go home and get dry. Some of her classmates are even passing out almost-dry towels from the locker room.

Ana hangs her head, the rest of the world forgotten.

This was definitely not the way she wanted it to go today. Nope. Not. At. All.

2

After the last diploma is handed out, the field looks like a giant green sink with grape soda swirling down its drain. The muddy grass only adds to the mess. Everyone's milling around in their graduation gowns, trying to find friends and family before the end of Life As They Know It. Ana doesn't need to mill. She knows where she's going. Straight toward Jamie Tabata. The way she sees it, she's got less than five minutes to get there before her family catches up to her and drags her home for Quality Time and a Family Feast. Time that will seem like a life sentence, and food that will taste like ash if she can't get rid of this one question, the one she's been choking on since the beginning of the school year. Less than five minutes to find out if she'll ever have any chance with Jamie Tabata.

"Ana! Ana!" The shout sounds like the crowd at a ticker tape parade. Ana ducks down. That would be her mom's mom, Grandma White, whose voice carries through a crowd after all those years as a schoolteacher. In a half crouch, holding the hem of her graduation gown so it doesn't get muddy, Ana scurries toward her destiny.

Jamie's standing at the side of the stage with his parents and Principal Rubens, who is nodding like a bird looking at its own reflection. Ana can imagine the conversation, all about Jamie's sparkling future and how he'll do so well in his new special private high school. Ana's step gets a little bouncier. Anyone would love to escape that chat. He'll be glad to see her.

She resumes a normal walk a few feet from her goal.

"Hey, Tabata," she says far more casually than she thought she could.

"Shen," he practically shouts, and grabs her elbow, stepping away from his folks. Mr. Tabata is a tall, handsome Japanese man in a gray suit, with a black tie. He gives Ana a sidelong glance but doesn't say anything. Principal Rubens is pumping his hand in farewell. Ana can't help noticing how much Jamie looks like his dad. Not bad, even when he's old, not bad at all.

"Sign my yearbook?" Ana asks, and hands the purple-bound album to Jamie.

"Sure. I'll trade you." He hands her his own yearbook. "Great speech, by the way."

9

Ana smirks. "Yeah, thanks. There were supposed to be fireworks, too, but I guess the timing was off."

Jamie laughs. "That was crazy."

"No kidding. I thought we were having an earthquake."

"Everyone did. Did you see the piece of roof that landed in the parking lot?"

"Really? Wow."

They stand there for moment, staring at the ruined roof of the gym.

"Sucks about the dance, though," Jamie says. He's looking at her when he says it. Ana blushes and looks at her feet.

"Yeah. So, um, I was wondering . . . is it true you're going to Crossroads next year?"

"Yeah." Jamie doesn't look too happy about it. "My dad says private's the way to go to get ready for college."

"That's too bad," Ana says. "I mean . . . since so many of us are going to University High instead."

Jamie's face falls. "I know. It's kind of crummy."

Ana takes a deep breath. *Say something now or regret it for the rest of your life.* "Well, um . . . Are you around this summer?"

Jamie's eyes widen in surprise. "Uh . . ." He stammers. Ana's stomach wobbles. Then she sees them. Her family, like the seven horsemen of the apocalypse, inexorably pushing their way toward her through the crowd. She panics and her mouth goes into overdrive. *They cannot be here for this.*

"Well, I just thought maybe sometime you'd like to, I dunno, maybe catch a mo—"

"Ah, James, there you are. Very rude to disappear like that." Ana sees Jamie flinch. His parents have found them before Ana can even finish her sentence. Mr. Tabata frowns at Jamie. It's clear Jamie gets his height from his mom, who comes up to Mr. Tabata's pinstriped elbow. Mrs. Tabata says nothing, just nods slightly in greeting. Ana's heart feels a little squeeze of empathy, like she suddenly has X-ray vision into the Tabata family, and now she likes Jamie even more.

"Sorry, Dad. I was just—" Jamie begins, when something tan and leggy bursts onto the scene.

"Jamie, there you are," says Amanda Conrad, the tallest, blondest girl in class.

"Hi, Mandy."

Mandy? *Mandy?* He only ever uses Ana's last name, but he's got a pet name for Amanda Conrad? Ana wants to gag. Worse, Mr. Tabata, who hasn't even batted an eye in Ana's direction, suddenly smiles.

"Miss Conrad, you were right, he was hiding over here."

Hiding? Ana feels like she's hiding too, right in plain sight. "Actually, he was talking to me," she says. "Ana Shen. Salutatorian."

She can't believe she said it, like it's a real title. Like Special Agent Shen, FBI. She puts her hand out anyway, and Mr. Tabata shakes it like it's a gag toy that might fall off in his hand any second.

"Ah yes, the girl on the stage when the water main blew. Pleasure, Miss Shen. Congratulations." Somehow he makes it sound like it was her fault.

"Thanks." She puts on her biggest smile.

Jamie smiles at Ana. She grins back at everyone. But "Mandy" will not be denied. She tosses her hair, eclipsing Ana's brown moon-face, like some sort of Greek goddess in her miraculously dry purple robe. The same robe that makes Ana look like the jelly half of a PB&J sandwich.

"Oh, hi, Ana. Nice hair."

Ana's grin loses some wattage. "Yeah, you should really try it yourself sometime. *Mandy*."

"Mandy" ignores her.

"Jamie," Amanda says in a suddenly girly and high-pitched voice. "You *are* coming to Abby's for pizza tonight, right? Everyone will be there." She grabs Jamie's arm and not too subtly squeezes his bicep. She's so tall she blocks out the sun. Behind Jamie, Mr. Tabata smiles again. Clearly, "Mandy" wins the parents' choice award.

Ana wishes she had a slingshot and an army of Philistines to witness her awesome accuracy as she beans Amanda right between her flashing Greek goddess eyes.

Jamie staggers under the weight of All That Is Amanda. "Um . . . I dunno. My folks are taking me out."

Ana involuntarily folds her arms. "Mandy" Conrad is a total sea cow.

"Well, Jamie," Mr. Tabata practically purrs, "we

might be persuaded to join your friends, if they're all as charming as Miss Conrad."

Jamie's eyes dart to Ana. Those eyes might be asking for help. Or they might be saying, *Hit the bricks, dork, I've got a real woman knocking at my door.* Ana frowns. Girl Scouts never offered a badge in how to read boys.

Suddenly, Chelsea appears at Ana's elbow.

"Ana, your family's here. What's up, Jamie?"

"Ana Mei Shen, you stay right there!" Ana flinches. Jamie glances toward the sound. One of the grandmothers has spotted her in the crowd. The horsemen ride toward her with purpose. As if Operation Failed Crush could get any more embarrassing.

"We're going to Abby's for pizza," Amanda Conrad announces in a singsong voice.

Chelsea raises an eyebrow. "Really? I heard they got shut down. Rats or something, right, Ana?"

"What?"

Ana hesitates. She grits her teeth and gives Chelsea a "cut it out" look. It doesn't work.

"Abby's. Got shut down, you told me yesterday. Yeah, that's why we're going to Ana's house for dinner. Big party planned. Tons of food. Ana makes these awesome dumpling things, right, Ana?"

"Pot stickers," Ana says automatically.

"Right. It's her specialty." Chelsea winks at Ana and tucks an arm through hers. "Jamie, you should totally come."

Oh dear God, Ana thinks. *What is Chelsea doing?*

"Sounds fun," Jamie says. "Dad? Can I?"

Mr. Tabata doesn't look as convinced as Jamie. In fact, he's not even looking at them, but at something coming their way. Ana glances around. Her family will be here any second. This was a mistake.

"I thought we'd spend time together . . . ," Mr. Tabata says slowly.

"Oh, it's totally a family thing," Chelsea says quickly. "Yeah, even *my* dad will be there. It's totally cool."

Ana barely hears her over the pounding in her own head. "Look, my fam . . . well, I should go." She looks down at the yearbook she's holding. Her hands are shaking. "Oh . . . um. Hey, let me sign this later."

She shoves it back at Jamie. And then she sees the look on Amanda Conrad's face.

"Actually . . ." Ana takes back the yearbook and scribbles her address inside it. "Dinner's at . . . six-thirty. See you there?"

Jamie grins. "Yeah. Great. I love pot stickers."

Ana returns the grin. "Great."

"Well, see you later!" Chelsea chirps, and squeezes Ana's arm. Ana glances back toward her family. The Shens are getting closer. Nai Nai, her father's mother, is in the lead, an imperious Chinese woman in an impeccable suit. Ana's mom, slim, brown, and decked out in a pantsuit she hand-painted, comes flowing after her. Mr. Tabata frowns and places a protective hand on Jamie's shoulder.

"See you later," Ana says.

Jamie reaches out and takes her hand. It's a second before she realizes he's shaking it good-bye. What a second. A full second of thinking he's just holding her hand. It feels warm. She hopes he can't tell she's blushing.

"Bye." Chelsea is tugging at her. They walk back into the crowd and—*wham!*

Ana's tackled full-force by her five-year-old brother. They hit the ground in a heap. "Sammy! God! Get off me!"

"Wheeee!" Sammy says with a giggle as Ana's dad drags him away. Somebody helps her to her feet. She hopes it's Jamie, but he's gone, blocked out by the forest of relatives.

3

"There's our girl!" It's Grandpa White, Ana's mother's dad. He looks handsome in a sport coat and lemonade-colored polo shirt that makes his skin look the same shade as a Dove chocolate bar. He pulls Ana into a hug.

"Grandpa." She hugs him back, wishing she could disappear into his shirt. "Thanks," she tells him, and dusts off the back of her gown.

"Ana, Ana, you did not give your speech! That Japanese boy goes first and *pow!*" Nai Nai says. Nai Nai (that means "father's mother" in Mandarin) tosses her hands into the air for emphasis. "He probably planned it. To prove he is smarter than you." Ana's stomach goes south. Nai Nai has a special knack for insulting greetings.

Ana's got what her social sciences teacher calls a "marvelously biracial, multicultural" family. Ana's social sciences teacher is a bit of a freak. What Ana really has is a Chinese American father and an African American mom. Those are the bi-races. Calling them cultural or marvelous is a stretch, in Ana's opinion. But that usually depends on the day.

"Hi, Nai Nai," Ana sighs.

Nai Nai turns to Ana's grandfather, whom Ana calls Ye Ye. "I told you second would be trouble. Better to be last than be number two." She turns back to Ana. "See? You should have worked harder."

Ana closes her eyes so she won't get snapped at for rolling them. "Like that would've kept the pipes from blowing up," she mutters to Chelsea. "Help me out?"

"Hi, Mr. Shen, hi, Mrs. Shen," Chelsea chimes in. While greetings and congratulations are exchanged, Ana looks over her shoulder and gets one last glimpse of Jamie. Tonight has to be perfect.

Unfortunately, her family is far from that. All the immediates are there: her mom's parents, newly flown in from Louisiana; her dad's parents, who drove up from Orange County for the day; her own parents, and the tackling menace that is her little brother, Matthew, nicknamed Sammy or the Samoan, after his favorite Girl Scout cookie. The fact that Sammy is wearing leaves where his clip-on tie should be only punctuates the complete lack of perfection. Ana stifles a sigh.

"Congratulations, graduate." Ana's mom pulls her

into a hug and kiss. She's beautiful, in Ana's somewhat biased opinion. She's willowy without being super-tall, and the tiny curls that make Ana's hair a nightmare look fun and carefree on her mom's head. Her mom is an artist, the locally-known-if-not-famous Helen White Shen, and it shows in the hand-painted silk pantsuit and tinkling bangles around her wrists.

"Thanks, Mom."

"And don't worry," her mother adds with a hard look at Nai Nai. "We've heard you practice your speech a thousand times. It was terrific."

"Yeah, tiger, good job," her dad says. "You too, Chelsea. Congratulations." Ana's dad is not an artist. He's an architect. Tall and lean, he's dressed almost the same as Jamie Tabata's dad—charcoal suit, white shirt. But there's no tie, the shirt is open at the collar, and he looks . . . comfortable. Ana and her dad exchange a complicated handshake that ends in a hug.

"Daniel, this is a school, not a clubhouse," Nai Nai says. Ana's dad shakes his head and gives the same complicated handshake to his father. Everyone is surprised when Ye Ye keeps up. Ye Ye is the old man of the family. Older than even Grandpa White. Ana's heard family rumors that he even fought in World War II, which makes him like the History Channel or something.

"That woman!" Grandma White mutters with a shake of her head. "Hi, baby. Congratulations." Grandma White is neatly dressed in a pantsuit and with matching purse and jewelry. Her graying hair is done up in perfect curls.

Ana knows she spends all day at the salon for special occasions.

"Hi, Grandma." Ana goes in for her tenth hug of the day. "Thanks for flying all the way out for this. Sorry it was so cruddy."

Her grandmother swats her with her purse. "Cruddy? How could my grandbaby's graduation ever be cruddy? Muddy, maybe"—she gives a throaty chuckle—"but never cruddy. And how are you, Miss Chelsea? Are you going to come out to dinner with us tonight? Ana's got a restaurant all picked out, in the Valley somewhere." Grandma White leans toward Chelsea conspiratorially. "She won't let us eat around here anymore. I think we embarrass her." She winks.

Ana and Chelsea exchange looks. Ana gets a little twinge in her stomach. "Uh . . . about that—"

"Can we go now?" Sammy interrupts. "I'm hungry."

"Sure, honey, let's go." Ana's mom takes the lead, sorting out the carpool situation. Grandma and Grandpa White will go with Ana's dad and brother in the SUV with their luggage. Ana, her mom and the Grandparents Shen will take the station wagon.

"Come along, young man. You and I can make sandwiches at home," Grandpa White says.

Sammy takes his grandfather by the hand. "I don't want a sandwich."

"Well, how about a 'samwich'?"

Sammy giggles.

"You guys go on," Ana says weakly. "I'll catch up in a

minute." She and Chelsea wait until her family is too far away to hear them.

Ana turns on her friend. "Oh my God, Chelsea. What did you just make me do?"

Chelsea's wicked grin belies her innocent shrug. "Don't blame me, blame Cupid. And don't worry. I'll come over at six to help out."

"Help out? Haven't you helped enough already?" Ana huffs. "Like my family's not enough of a sideshow, now I've got to introduce them all to Jamie? And his dad? Blech."

"Oh, don't pretend to be angry. You wanted pizza with Jamie, and now you get to have him in your actual house for a whole evening. And your family gets what they want too. Dinner with their precious grandbaby. What more could you possibly ask for?"

Ana's scowl melts into a grudging half-grin. "Not much, I guess. But . . . wait a minute. That means we have to cook! We haven't had a meal at home with all my grandparents in five years!"

Chelsea shrugs. "But your grandmothers can cook. You're always talking about your grandma's gumbo, and like I told Jamie, those dumpling things you made that time were really good."

"Pot stickers." Ana sighs. "Yeah, they're good, but mine are all lumpy and funny-looking."

"Hey, you said they were supposed to look like that," Chelsea complains.

Ana blushes. "Well, they're not. And Jamie knows it.

He *likes* them! And he's gonna know *I* made them! Ugh." She tosses her head back and gasps up at the sky. "And my grandmothers! Geez, Chelsea, you don't know my grandmothers."

"Um, friends since second grade, yeah, I do," Chelsea replies.

"No, really," Ana says. "We've had exactly three family meals with both sides together." She ticks them off on her fingers. "Thanksgiving right after my parents got married, Nai Nai said the turkey was dry and raw at the same time. My mom burst into tears and spent the night driving around the block with a bucket of chicken strips she was too embarrassed to serve. Christmas when I was five, Nai Nai cooked an exotic Mandarin feast complete with ducks' feet and fungus for dessert. Grandpa White ended up in the emergency room with a bad MSG reaction, and my mom sent me to bed with a can of Vienna sausages. And then we tried it one last time when Sammy was born. Grandma White offered to cook, since my mom was coming home from the hospital. She never even turned on the stove. Between her and Nai Nai, we ended up with takeout.

"We eat out together. We *have* to eat out together, or else there'll be a fight or a disaster or the end of the world. It was a miracle to have Nai Nai and Grandma White on the same sports field, let alone in the same kitchen."

Ana sighs. "This is no longer a dinner, it's a competition. That means you've just made my life hell for the next"—she glances at her watch—"four hours. Four hours! Holy crap, I've gotta go! And look at my hair! And that's, like, twelve people to feed."

Chelsea winces. "Fifteen."

"What?"

"I told Mr. Tabata my family would be there, remember? That was the clincher."

"Right." Ana groans.

"I know," Chelsea replies. "I've gotta get Chuck cleaned up and presentable."

"Stop calling him Chuck, he's your dad."

"Hey, us children of divorce have to grow up fast," Chelsea counters. Ana rolls her eyes.

"You're a child of trial separation, not divorce."

Chelsea sighs. "Yeah, whatever. Don't you have shopping to do? For Jamie?" She draws the *a* in his name out and wiggles her eyebrows. Ana laughs, and this time her smile lingers.

"Right." She takes a deep breath and hugs Chelsea. "See you tonight."

"Sure thing." The girls separate, backing away from each other across the muddy lawn.

"And don't forget, if you start to freak out . . ." Chelsea holds her hand to her head like a phone. "Call me," she mouths.

Ana mimics the movement and gives a thumbs-up and a cheesy wink. It's the last smile she shares at Edison Junior High. Then she runs.

2

Mud and running do not mix. Ana goes dashing across the swampy part of the field, menus for tonight's dinner flashing through her head. The flood in the school gymnasium is draining slowly into the parking lot. They've even brought in pumps to speed up the job. Ana is moving so fast she hits the asphalt before she can stop herself. And it's six inches under water. If her graduation gown didn't run before, it does now. Purple dye splashes everywhere. She hops on tiptoe out of the puddle and runs, crablike, to where her family is waiting beside her mother's station wagon.

"Grandma! Grandma!" She comes skidding to a halt in front of her family.

"—but otherwise, it was a nice flight," Grandma White finishes saying to Ana's dad. Then, slowly, deliberately, she turns and gives Ana a hard look. "Young lady, where is the fire?"

Ana takes a deep breath, her fingers tingling with embarrassment. "Sorry, Grandma. I was . . . it's just that— will you make your gumbo for dinner?"

Grandma White's expression melts into a proud smile. "Why, of course, baby girl. I'd be glad to. You hear that, Derby, she's asking for my home cooking on her big day."

Grandpa White grins and puts his arm around his wife. "Sure she is, honey. That's the kind of food that brings hope to the hopeless. Good eating."

"I thought we were eating out," Sammy whines, tugging on Grandpa White's leg.

"We're not eating out?" Ye Ye asks, his hooded eyes opening in surprise. He looks at Nai Nai and Ana's dad.

Ana winces. No jobs for her at the United Nations.

"What I meant was . . . well, Chelsea and I . . . we kind of invited a couple of people over for dinner, and it would really mean a lot to me if we didn't have to disinvite them."

Another surprised silence follows. Ana's shoulders rise and lock together before she can stop them.

"Well, we could still eat out," her dad says hopefully.

"No? Not really?" Ana's voice rises into a question and she winces even more. This is not the way she planned it. Then again, nothing's gone the way she planned today. Today is her big day. Ask and she should have received.

But she didn't ask right and now she's stuck in wince mode, eyes scrunched in anticipation of disaster.

Grandma White clutches her purse imperiously. Nai Nai purses her lips imperiously. Ye Ye and Grandpa White shrug. Ana's dad puts an arm around her mother's shoulders. Her mother sighs and looks down at the ground.

"Oh, Ana, honey. Look at your legs," her mother says.

Ana looks down. Zebra stripes of purple are spiraling their way down her calves.

Ana closes her eyes. "No, no, no, no, no." *Jamie Tabata is coming over tonight and I look like a leper,* she thinks. *Get a grip, get a grip.*

The Samoan starts to laugh. "Ana's got tights on, Ana's got tights on."

Nai Nai clucks her tongue. Ana swears under her breath. At least the attention is off dinner for a minute.

"Hold on, baby." It's Grandma White, rummaging through her giant purse. "I've got something in here . . ."

"Just pull it off me," Ana pleads, struggling with the gown.

"What, over that fine head of hair?" her grandmother asks. "No, hold still."

Right, thinks Ana. Nothing a shower and a lot of hair gel wouldn't improve.

A small pair of sewing scissors flashes in the sunlight, and Ana's grandmother cuts the gown straight down the back.

"What are you doing?" Ana shrieks.

"There, now take it off."

"Mom!" Ana's mom grabs the sleeves from the front and Ana pulls her arms free. At least she's out of the gown. She looks down. Her pale pink graduation dress is ruined, speckled and stained with purple dye, like an Easter egg with the shell removed. "I look like I'm contagious."

"Don't worry, there's a towel in the way-back." Her mom goes to rummage through the back of the car. Ana follows for a quick toweling off, removing most of the dye from her arms and legs. Afterward, she takes a seat on the tailgate to take off her mucky sandals. Her mom stands in front of her, and they each take a muddy shoe to clean.

"So," her mother says now that they're alone. "What's going on with you and Chelsea?"

Ana blushes. "Nothing. We just thought, since there's no dance, we could have dinner together . . . with some friends."

Ana's mom quirks an eyebrow. "How many friends?"

Ana blushes even more. Mr. Tabata doesn't exactly count as a friend, but . . . "Um, six?"

Ana's mom shakes her head. Ana knows what she's thinking. Christmas, Thanksgiving and Sammy's first day home . . . not exactly a good track record.

Her mom sighs and drops her shoulders. "Well, who knows? Maybe the fourth time will be the charm for us. We might have to set up in the backyard, though."

Ana breathes a sigh of relief. "Cool. It should be fun."

Her mother looks up from the sandal she's cleaning. "Fun? Huh. I've never heard you use that word when it comes to family dinners."

Ana shrugs. "Well, I know that, when it's just us, and Grandma and Nai Nai get into it or whatever. But it'll be different this time, since we'll have company. Right?"

"Who knows," her mom says, rising and handing over the cleaned shoe. "Maybe *Family Feud* will skip a round. It's a nice thought." Ana accepts the kiss her mother plants on her forehead. "Well, honey, you'd better go ask Nai Nai to cook too, or we'll never hear the end of it."

Ana puts her shoes on and checks her reflection out in the window. Not bad, for a sponge bath and a speckled dress.

Ana's mom smoothes out the back of Ana's dress. "Boy, this Jamie kid better be worth it."

Ana's jaw drops. Her mom just winks. "It's okay. Kind of obvious, the way you two were looking at each other onstage."

"It was? I mean . . . he was giving me a look?"

Her mom smiles and shrugs. "It might have been a look. Or something. Just don't tell your dad. He'll lock you in your closet until you're eighteen."

Ana shakes her head. "Twenty-one. He already told me."

"Well, his bark is worse than his bite," her mom says.

Ana turns to rejoin the rest of the family, and stops. "Thanks, Mom."

Her mom smiles. "That's what I'm here for."

Everyone else is waiting patiently by the front of the car. "Nai Nai?" Ana approaches her father's parents. Nai

Nai seems to be counting the leaves on the eucalyptus tree towering over their heads. If she were a cartoon, there would be fuming little angry-lines waving over her head.

"Yes? Did you say something?"

Ana takes a deep breath. "Grandmother, it would be an honor if you would prepare a special dish for tonight's festivities," she says painstakingly in Mandarin. Ana is by no means fluent, but with each word she manages, Nai Nai's face, if it doesn't exactly smile, at least softens.

At last, Nai Nai nods. "How else was it going to be a party?" She flings a hand toward Grandma White. "You think a little bowl of soup is enough to feed guests? Of course not. This is a banquet. We need eight dishes—no, nine is more auspicious. Yuan, get me a pen." She taps Ye Ye on his arm. Ana's grandfather obediently pats his pockets until he comes up with a small notepad and paper.

"I will make a list," Nai Nai says, and begins jotting down her thoughts in quick Chinese characters. "This is my granddaughter's special day. I will make it the best."

"Oh, I'll do dumplings," Ana adds. "And *lu bo gao* would be good." Sweet and salty turnip cakes speckled with shrimp and Chinese sausage. The thought of them makes Ana's mouth water.

Nai Nai pauses. "Who's planning this party, anyway?"

Ana snatches the pad and pen away. "We are, of course." She waves her arm to gather her family closer.

"Okay, so we've got dumplings and *lu bo gao,* gumbo and lion's head, fried rice, what else? Dessert? Anyone?"

Ana's mom raises her hand. "I was going to make a cake anyway. I'll make it a little bigger."

"Great, Mom. Grandpa, do you want to contribute?"

Grandpa White shakes his head. "Do you have to ask? My world-famous chicken has got to be on the menu of any party where the guest of honor is my grand-daughter."

"Sounds good to me." Ana jots it down on her pad. "So that's"—she counts in her head, lips moving—"that's eight dishes. Who wants to do the ninth?"

Nai Nai steps forward and snatches the list from Ana. "Hey!" Ana cries.

"I will do the ninth. We must be orderly. We must make a shopping list. We must be clear, or mistakes will be made. Right, Mrs. White?"

Ana shudders. Nai Nai always insists on being formal with Ana's other grandmother. Ana's dad says it's a matter of pride—the *via* in *Olivia* trips up Nai Nai's tongue and turns into *Oliver*. It still irks Grandma White, though. Especially since Grandpa White is on a first-name basis with both Nai Nai and Ye Ye.

Fortunately, this afternoon, Grandma White doesn't take the bait. She simply nods and says, "That's sound advice. Sound advice indeed." Nai Nai doesn't even see her shake her head, or mutter, "That woman!"

"Great," Ana says with a sigh of relief. "Now, write your lists and let's go shopping!" She all but claps her hands like a chirpy camp counselor.

Ana's dad hauls Sammy up onto his shoulders. "Saddle up, cowboys. First stagecoach to Ralph's, head this way!" The Grandparents White and Sammy go with Ana's dad to his SUV. Ye Ye follows.

"The SUV has a television," he says by way of apology, and shuffles away.

Ana looks at her mom and Nai Nai. Not the best arrangement, but it will have to do. Ana's mother takes a deep breath.

"Pavilion?" she asks, naming the nearest grocery chain. "There's one a few blocks from here."

Nai Nai shakes her head and gets into the station wagon. "Monterey Park is better. I'll tell you where to drive."

Ana drops down in the middle seat of the wagon. She shuts the door, and suddenly, everything sinks in. This is her last day at Edison Junior High. Ana feels like the life is being pulled out of her, down the length of her arms, through the tips of her fingers and toes. She is tired, bone tired. That's a Grandma White phrase, and it fits. Maybe it was getting up early for the ceremony. Maybe it was staying up all night trying to perfect her speech. Or anticipating the graduation dance. Or running from the great flood. Or maybe it's just plain depression. Now it's over. Anything can happen at dinner tonight, but after that, who knows?

Everything's changing, she thinks. She's said good-bye to her grade-school friends, to all her old teachers, to the principal, and now here she is, in the backseat of her mom's blue station wagon, head resting against the window, letting the vibrations of the 405 freeway drum away a small, small feeling of regret.

"How do you feel?" her mom asks. Nai Nai is surprisingly quiet in the front seat. No doubt planning her next salvo.

Ana sighs. "Different."

Ana's mother smiles at her in the rearview mirror, a very faint smile. "Now you're growing up."

Ha, Ana thinks. *Maybe I can start calling my parents Dan and Helen.*

In the front seat, Nai Nai's breath catches in one quick sob.

Ana closes her eyes. That's why everyone's so quiet, she realizes. Ana the little girl no longer exists. *Now, that's depressing. I'm growing up and I haven't even kissed a boy. Not one that's counted, anyway.*

Ana lapses back into her thoughts and lets the hum of the car's wheels lull her. By the time they reach the part of the freeway that looks across downtown Los Angeles, she's fast asleep.

5

Ana wakes up in the station wagon, in the parking lot of the Monterey Park 99 Ranch Market. Her face is hot from the sun. She shakes her head. "Where's Nai Nai?"

"Inside," her mom says. "Good grief. I cannot find a space here. It's like the whole world's shopping today." Ana looks around and sees that they're idling behind a line of other searching cars. Ana catches her mom watching her in the rearview mirror.

"You all right, honey?" her mom asks.

Ana sighs. "Yeah. I guess I kind of wish I'd gotten to read my speech." Her mother frowns. Ana wants to smooth away the little furrow between her mother's brows. She leans over the front seat and kisses her mom on the forehead.

Her mother chuckles. "I thought it went very well. Even the water show. You're too hard on yourself sometimes, Ana. Today's your day. Relax."

Ana collapses back into her seat. Even with the AC on, the sun is heating up the car through the windshield. She lowers her window. "My day, right."

"Don't tell me you're not looking forward to tonight."

"I guess." It's hard to sort out the anxiety from the excitement, Ana realizes. She leans back, looking at the ceiling of the station wagon. The thin, fuzzy cloth is starting to sag in pale blue waves.

The car has moved five inches in the past five minutes.

"Come on!" her mom mutters, tapping the steering wheel in frustration. The cars ahead of them roll another two inches. "Your grandmother is going to give me hell for this one." She talks to Ana over her shoulder. "Hon, will you please go in there and help her? I swear she'll think we've driven off and left her behind." Ahead of them, the lane is a row of taillights surrounded by a wall-to-wall carpet of sports cars and old sedans, Asian families pressing through the rows with shopping carts in front of them. "Why did I agree to take her here?" Ana's mom shakes her head and sighs.

Ana squeezes her mother's shoulder as she sits up. None of them would be here if it weren't for Chelsea's big mouth and Ana's small one.

"I'll go." Ana yawns. "I"—she stretches and yawns

through her words—"need (yawn) dumpling (yawn) stuff too." She opens the door.

Her mother turns around and gives her a smile. "That's my girl. You know how to deal with Nai Nai." She reaches out and pats Ana's hand. "Tonight will be fine. I promise. Now go find your grandmother."

Going into the 99 Ranch Market is like stepping into a grocery store on the other side of the planet. Ana stretches her arms over her head, suppresses another yawn and lets it turn into a smile. She loves it when Nai Nai takes her here. Being in the Chinese market is like leaving Los Angeles for an hour, like leaving the whole United States. The spicy scents of ginger and pepper float through the air, along with the faded ocean scent of seaweed, and stranger smells, like dried shark fin, with its musty parchment and bouillon scent. It's strangely comforting to feel so transported. Like there isn't a whole crowd about to descend on your house, like the boy you have the hots for isn't about to come over and maybe, just maybe, make your summer worthwhile.

Ana grabs a small basket and heads toward the produce section. The eggplant alone comes in more shapes and sizes than in an American market. Ana walks past the speckled purple and green shapes to the bin of ginger-root. For the number of dumplings she's got to make, three per person for fourteen people . . . that's forty-two dumplings. That's one and a half batches. Ana picks up a small piece of the gnarled tan root and takes a sniff.

"Blech." She puts it back and looks for a fresher piece. Ana's favorite dish is dumplings—it's the only thing she can make without a recipe. So what if she hasn't quite got a handle on shaping them? Nai Nai and her dad make it look so easy: a flat circle of dough in one palm; stuff, fold and pinch with the other hand. Ana shakes her head. She wasn't kidding when she said hers come out funny. Maybe her hands are too small or something, but it doesn't matter. Today they have to be perfect.

She goes through several knobs of ginger before finding the one. It smells peppery-sweet and fresh. More than enough to add a lot of flavor to the pot stickers, and plenty left over for the dipping sauce of soy sauce, sesame oil and vinegar.

She spends almost as much time finding the crispest Napa cabbage she can. Except for the ground pork, they should have the rest of the ingredients back at home.

Halfway down the next row, Ana sees the smiling faces and flowery packaging that say she's in the toiletries aisle. She pauses to pick up a bar of soap that claims to be made of ground pearls. It smells like Ivory and a hint of fake flowers. She puts it back on the shelf and moves into the shampoo section.

"Sunset Gold™." Ana stops. She's in front of the hair dye, a solid row of boxes bragging shades of hair, from blond to red, and a few deep browns and blacks. Sunset Gold™ is the most striking.

Ana glances up and down the aisle. She's alone. She picks up the box.

The girl on the package could be Amanda Conrad, tall and slim with waist-length honey-colored hair cascading over her shoulders. Except that here at 99 Ranch Market, the model on the box is Chinese.

The thing is, the color looks good on her. Her almond skin looks exotic beneath the deep blond hair. Her face looks . . . mysterious.

Ana turns the package over, her basket forgotten at her feet, free hand reaching for her own dark curls, now completely undone from her haphazard braiding.

Ana drops the box into her basket and hurries off to find Nai Nai.

Halfway to the butcher counter, she stops to look at the bruise-colored chicken in the poultry case beneath the sign that declares it BLACK CHICKEN. "Huh. That's new," she says to herself.

"That makes good soup," Nai Nai says over her shoulder. Nai Nai's bracelets jingle as she reaches past Ana to grab a pound of the blue-skinned meat. "It's good for the blood."

"I was just looking for you," Ana says. "Mom's still trying to find a parking spot." She hands her grandmother the shopping list and kisses her on her delicately powdered cheek. Nai Nai gives her cart-pushing duty. Ana puts her shopping basket in with her grandmother's groceries.

"Thank you, dear. Now, help me find the meat man. I want my pork ground fresh."

Ana rings the bell for the butcher. Her grandmother frowns at the young guy who comes out from the back. He can't be more than twenty-five, with a pierced eyebrow and hair that's been bleached auburn.

"How is your pork?" Nai Nai asks him in Mandarin. The butcher tells her it's good. Nai Nai looks surprised.

"Oh, you speak Chinese, do you? With hair like that, I didn't know." She orders her meat, ground medium so there's more fat in the mix. While he works, Nai Nai turns to Ana, who is fiddling with a package of pigs' ears.

"See, he speaks Chinese pretty well for a kid your age."

Ana runs a finger along a pig ear's edge, feeling the cartilage. She shakes her head. "He's not my age, Nai Nai. And I speak better Chinese than Dad."

Nai Nai flushes beneath her face powder. "Well, you'll speak it even better when you come back from Taiwan."

Ana tweaks the ear and puts it back in the case. "Right, one day."

Ana's grandmother takes the package of pork from the young butcher with a nod.

Ana sighs, shaking her head. Nai Nai always talks about taking Ana and her cousins to Taiwan. Ana herself has only been once, when she was a toddler, and that was with her parents.

Nai Nai turns toward the butcher and says in English, "This is my granddaughter. She just graduated first in her class."

Ana grits her teeth. "Second, Nai Nai. Second." The butcher is smiling at her in a way that says he's got a grandmother like Nai Nai, too. A woman who would rob him of his only chance at dating and kidnap him during the last summer he might ever spend with his best friend for the sake of a few language lessons.

"She she," Ana thanks him in Mandarin, and quickly pushes the grocery cart away. Nai Nai follows, unfazed.

At the checkout counter, Ana slips the box of hair coloring in with the rest of the groceries. Nai Nai is too busy to notice.

"Do not shortchange me," she admonishes the cashier, a gum-chewing Chinese girl a couple of years older than Ana.

"This celery is a day old," Nai Nai says, shaking the wilted leaves at the girl. "It shouldn't be full price."

"I'll have to call the manager, ma'am," the girl says with a half-yawn.

Nai Nai clutches her purse and pulls herself upright. All five foot three inches of her.

"You do that. I'll wait."

"Oh God," Ana moans to herself. Behind them, the growing line heaves a collective sigh. Ana turns around to give them an apologetic smile and immediately looks away.

It's like Nai Nai has been cloned. Five older women, each with a death grip on her handbag and an unsatisfactory piece of produce, make up the rest of the line.

"Manager to register two," the girl says over the intercom.

The poor man who shows up turns pale at the sight of

the women. He pats his clip-on tie and straightens his short-sleeve dress shirt before assuming a fixed smile.

"Ladies," he says in placating Mandarin. "The produce truck was delayed. But we are having a sale! Half off on everything."

"Everything?" Nai Nai asks in English.

The manager's eyes flicker across the checkout lines. Ana tries not to smile. By speaking English, Nai Nai has just extended the discount to the handful of teens and non-Asians in the line as well. And the manager knows it.

He actually breaks into a sweat. "On produce, yes," he says, also in English.

Nai Nai shrugs and nods.

"So. Okay."

The manager's shoulders relax and the line moves forward again.

In all the drama, Ana's hair dye goes unnoticed at the checkout stand. She pulls it out of the bag on the way to the car and tucks it into her graduation gown. Purple or blond, by the time Jamie comes over, she'll be a total knockout.

6

"Here we are!" Ana's mother says brightly, pulling into the driveway. The SUV is already at the house, parked on the street. Ana gathers her graduation gown with the package of hair dye wrapped safely inside.

"I still say you should have exited at Centinela," Nai Nai insists. "It was a waste of time to take the freeway all the way. Your house is closer to Centinela."

"You might be right, Mei," Ana's mother says patiently. "I should time it on the next trip."

From where she's sitting, Ana can see her mother's hands gripping the steering wheel tight enough to crack it. Ana sits up to clear the air.

"Well, we're home now, Nai Nai," she says, and unlocks her door. "Time for you to work your kitchen magic." Ana's mother looks at her gratefully. "Come on, Mom. I'll help you with these groceries."

Ana hops out of the car, with the idea that if she moves fast enough, Nai Nai won't have time to argue.

"Next time, I'm driving my parents," Ana's mother says with a meaningful look at Nai Nai. Before Ana can respond, her mother kisses her on the forehead and shoves two bags of Chinese greens into her arms.

"You can carry more than that," Nai Nai says from the tailgate, and swings an entire chicken, head and all, toward Ana.

Ana learned long ago to ignore the instinct to duck. The bird is dead anyway. Poor thing. Now it's going to be soup. Nai Nai's soups are good enough to make Ana philosophical about the bird. She grabs another bag, this one containing warty green bitter melons, and stiff-legs it into the house, groceries slapping at her thighs.

Ana's house is one of a handful of two-story houses on a tree-lined block less than a mile from the ocean. The Shens' house was once a 1930s bungalow, but it was added on to until it became the top-heavy building it is today. As with most of the houses on the street, the backyard is much larger than the house and lies hidden behind a wall covered in jasmine vines. On certain days, Ana can smell the ocean's seaweed scent from the front steps. She likes to open her window to the breeze and, if she's lucky, in the late spring and summer, the scent of night-blooming jasmine from the front walk drifts inside. Today it's too warm for the ocean breeze, but the flowers are sure to open when the sun sets.

"Where's the Samoan?" Ana mutters. "Sammy, get out here!" She drops her bags on the faded vinyl floor of the eat-in kitchen and runs back up the hall and outside again, pausing to tuck her graduation gown with its box of hair dye under one arm. It's always better to help unload the car than it is to unpack the bags. Despite their differences, all three of the older women in Ana's family have a talent for buying exactly twice as many groceries as can actually fit in the refrigerator. How they ever pack the fridge and the freezer is a mystery. Ana wants nothing to do with it. Normally, she'd scurry away after unloading the car, but today she has to keep the peace. She sighs. No reason she has to do it alone.

"Sammy!" she calls out, carrying in another load. The Samoan does not show up. Neither does Ye Ye nor her dad.

"Great," she mutters, and grabs one last load of bags. This time, her mother and Nai Nai follow her.

"That's it, honey," her mom says, kicking the front door shut with her toe. "Want to help unpack?"

"Sure," Ana says, fighting another sigh. She throws open the kitchen door.

"Surprise!"

Ana almost drops her bags and stumbles back out the door.

Everyone is in the kitchen—Ye Ye, Grandpa and Grandma White, Ana's dad and Sammy. They've all changed out of their dress clothes and into T-shirts or polos, shorts and khakis, except for Grandma White, who is as coiffed and composed as ever. And all of them have goofy or smug smiles plastered across their faces.

Ana gives them an untrusting look. "What's going on?"

Ana's mom takes her bags from her.

"Happy graduation, kiddo," Ana's dad says. "Sit down, Madame Graduate. We've got some presents for you."

"Oh!" Ana relaxes. She scampers to the place of honor, one of the vinyl-cushioned chairs at their tatty old Formica kitchen table. Her parents bought it at the Pasadena Flea Market right after they got married. "It's a 1950s vintage dinette set," her dad would say, proud despite the faded gold sparkles set into the pot-scorched white tabletop.

Ana's dad pulls out her graduation cap and plunks it on her head.

"Painstakingly dried with a hair dryer," he explains. "So it's just like a birthday, but with a commemorative square hat."

"It's the birth of a smarter, more mature you," Ana's mom says. It sounds goofy, but Ana finds herself grinning.

"Our own little Ana Mei, strutting her stuff onstage!" Grandpa White exclaims. "You've got a whole future ahead of you, baby girl, full of opportunities your old grandparents never had."

Grandma White nods. "Head of her class."

"When we first came to the States, we could not even rent an apartment in this neighborhood," Nai Nai says. "And now here you are, standing up in front of everyone. It is very impressive." She shrugs. "Too bad about your speech."

Ana's grin fades. Her dad clears his throat. "It's gift time. The Samoan's the youngest, so he goes first."

On cue, Sammy pulls a small box wrapped in the Sunday comics page from under the table.

"Thank you, Sammy."

Sammy giggles. "You're welcome."

Ana starts to unwrap the box. "Don't tear it," Nai Nai says. "It's still good paper."

"It's newspaper, Ma," Ana's dad says. Nai Nai doesn't care. Ana's too happy to roll her eyes. She carefully peels back the tape and lets Nai Nai fold the paper up again.

Ana takes the lid off the box . . .

"A sock? Socks?" She lays them out on the kitchen table. Nine socks, none of them a matching pair.

"They're not socks, they're *puppets,*" Sammy explains. He pulls one onto his arm to demonstrate. Sure enough, the face unfolds, complete with eyes on the heel and a felt nose on the end of the toe.

"Cute." Ana slides one onto her own hand. "Hello, everybody," she says in a dopey puppet voice.

"He worked all week on those," Ana's mom explains.

"One for each of us," Sammy adds. "That's Nai Nai and Ye Ye, me and Mom, Dad, you and Grandma and Grandpa."

Ana can't say there's much resemblance, but she nods. "So who's the ninth sock supposed to be?"

Sammy shrugs. "It's just a sock. For your foot."

Ana laughs. "Thanks, Sammy." She gives him a hug and puts the sock family back in the box.

"Next," Ana's dad says. Her parents look at each other and her mom nods.

"Since you'll be starting high school in the fall and it's too far to walk, we got you—"

Ana's eyes widen. Her heart skips a beat. "A car?"

"No!" her mom says. "You're too young to drive."

"A scooter?" Ana asks.

"No." Her dad sighs and pulls a small envelope out of his pocket.

"A bus card?" The disappointment is more than a little obvious and she knows it. "I mean, hey, a bus card."

"It's a monthly pass," her dad adds lamely.

"I knew that one was a dud," Ana's mom says. "Your dad thought you wouldn't want us dropping you off at school anymore. Said we'd embarrass you."

"Yeah, I can see that." Ana nods. "Thanks, Dad. Good idea." She stands up and gives him a kiss.

"Wait, wait, wait," her mother says. "We also got you"—she pulls two cards from her shirt pocket—"gift cards for the mall and the movie theater."

Ana's eyes go wide again. "Hey, thanks, Mom! And Dad," she adds, hugging them both.

"You'll need your back-to-school wardrobe, after all," her mom says.

"Thanks." Ana sits back down with a satisfied sigh.

45

The day has taken a good turn. "Well, I guess I'll get started on the dumplings."

"Young lady, you are in some kind of a hurry," Grandma White admonishes. "You don't really think your own grandparents forgot about you on your big day?"

Ana blushes. "I didn't want to be greedy."

"Good girl," Grandpa White says. "You should be grateful every day. Honey, tell her what to be grateful for today."

Grandma White breaks into a smile. "Ana, remember those Mississippi steamboats you used to love so much?"

"Yeah," Ana says. *When I was, like, ten,* she thinks.

"Well, pack your bags, baby. Next month, we're taking you on a cruise! A musical heritage cruise down the Mississippi River, St. Louis to New Orleans. We'll even stop and meet some of your cousins and relations along the way."

"Um. Wow," Ana says. She suddenly feels split in two. Embarrassing as it is, the cruise sounds like fun. Not the uninterrupted summer full of Chelsea and Jamie Tabata she's been dreaming of, but she has to admit a trip to New Orleans is pretty cool. Especially a musical tour—Ana might only be second in her class, but she's the first chair alto saxophone in her school band.

"Wow." She says it again, this time with a smile. She looks at her parents. Her mom is grinning from ear to ear, and Ana is too. Her dad suddenly looks worried. Then Ana knows why. Nai Nai is whispering to Ye Ye rapidly in Chinese. *Oh dear God,* Ana thinks. *The bigger the grin now, the bigger it'll have to be for Nai Nai and Ye Ye's gift. Why does life have to be so complicated?*

"Don't look so worried, honey. You won't get seasick on those big old boats, I promise," Grandma White says. Ana smiles again but tries not to grin, and gives them each a hug. Grandpa White chuckles and pats her back.

"We know how much you like playing saxophone and all," he explains.

"Yeah. That does sound really cool," Ana admits.

"Our turn?" Ye Ye asks Ana's dad. He nods, the look of worry on his face poorly concealed.

Ye Ye smiles broadly and pulls a small red envelope from his pocket.

Ana smiles back. It is a *huen bao,* or red packet. Her father's parents have been slipping these to her on holidays ever since she was old enough to hold an envelope. When she was little, just the act of tearing it open made her smile. Now Ana blushes even thinking about it. *Huen bao* are gifts of money, the red envelope signifying good luck and prosperity.

Ana accepts the envelope with a little bow. *"She she,"* she says, thanking them in Mandarin. The envelope is stamped with a gold foil dragon wrapped around the name of her grandparents' bank. Some of the branches give the envelopes out during the Chinese New Year. Nai Nai probably hordes them by the handful each year.

"It is nothing great," Ye Ye says in his careful voice. "But we are very, very proud of you, Ana Mei."

Ana smiles and slips the envelope into her pocket. She

learned long ago that it's rude to open the little packet in front of the giver. She also learned that her grandparents always call it a small gift when it's usually very generous. Ana gets up and gives them each a hug and a kiss. Nai Nai still seems unhappy, but Ye Ye is unfazed.

"Perhaps you will use it on your trip down the Mississippi," he says amicably.

Ana smiles. "That'd be great. Maybe I can even put it toward a real New Orleans saxophone or something."

"Would you listen to that?" Grandma White says. "Isn't that nice? She's excited already."

"I told you she would be, Mama," Ana's mother says, and pats Grandma White on the shoulder.

Ana can't help feeling happy. "Thanks, everybody. This is really cool." She looks around the room, smiling. Everybody smiles back, even Nai Nai, although her smile is a little crooked. Ana shrugs inwardly. At least nobody's shouting.

"So, um, shouldn't we get cooking?" she asks, glancing at the clock. Three hours and counting. Her heart skips a beat.

Everybody moves at once.

"Do you want a sandwich, Ana?" her dad asks. "We had some PB&Js earlier."

"I don't think I can eat just yet," Ana says. Maybe it's butterflies left over from this morning's speech, or maybe it's Jamie's fault, but the thought of wasting one more precious peaceful family minute to have a sandwich kills any idea of eating before dinner.

"I'll start the dough for the pot stickers." Ana goes to the sink and washes her hands.

Her mother grips her shoulder. "You want to shower and change first?"

Ana kisses her mom on the cheek. "Right. Thanks, Mom. I'll hurry."

She runs for the stairs, cap in hand, brushing past the paintings and family photos her mother has hanging on the staircase wall.

"Stop running!" Nai Nai shouts after her. "Always rushing around like a horse, tromp tromp tromp. You are not a horse!"

7

Ana collapses on her bed. After a second, she gets up and locks her door. Swapping her dress for an oversized T-shirt, she lies back down, gazing up at the white popcorn ceiling. Sometimes at night, when the light from the street comes in just right, the ceiling twinkles like a galaxy of tiny stars.

Right now, it's just white with tacky flecks of silver here and there.

Ana's cell phone rings. She lets it ring twice before she realizes it's Chelsea's ring tone. "Hello?"

"Hey, need to escape yet?"

Ana smiles and relaxes again. "Nope. Surprisingly

quiet down there so far, but I'm hiding in my room. I've got to shower. My gown totally speckled me."

"I told you it would stain."

"But you didn't take out your little sewing scissors and cut it off me like my grandmother did."

"What? That's crazy."

"It was like her pocket version of the Jaws of Life. But hey, everything's cool with my folks as far as dinner goes. So it might even be under control. Still, come early if you can. I totally need help picking out what to wear."

"Alrighty. See you at six-ish."

"Bye."

Ana hangs up and rummages through her closet. Chelsea's the one with fashion sense. Ana gives up on choosing a dress. Work clothes now, adorable dress later.

Ana's room is the same shade of white it was when her parents bought the house after Sammy was born, but the walls are covered in music posters and pictures of places where Ana's been, or wants to go. There's a photo of a jazz quartet under the wrought-iron balconies of the French Quarter in New Orleans, a postcard of the New York skyline, a Chinese watercolor of strangely humped mountains over a river. Her mother claims it came from the village where Ye Ye was born, but Ana can't picture that. It's the only one in a proper frame, hung up with an actual nail. Beneath it, Ana's saxophone lies in the corner, nestled in its case, waiting for her to join her new high school's band.

"Enough lollygagging," she tells herself. She lays a

pair of shorts and a polo shirt out on the powder blue bedspread and pulls out the box of hair dye. She tucks it into the towel she keeps on the back of the door for her hair, and slips down the hall to the shower.

Ana sits on the edge of the tub, reading the label. Downstairs, she can hear her dad dragging the extra chairs from the dining room into the backyard. No fighting or screaming yet. She relaxes a little and reads the directions again.

" 'Apply to damp hair.' Well, I've certainly got that. 'Do not shampoo hair first. Leave in for ten minutes.' " Ana looks at her watch, then at the model on the package. From brown to blond in less than twenty minutes. Ana can just imagine it, descending the staircase, her brown curls transformed into a halo of Sunset Gold™.

"Nai Nai won't say anything embarrassing, at least," Ana tells herself. "She'll be dead from the shock."

She remembers Nai Nai's hints about taking her to Taiwan, and her stomach clenches. She puts the bottle down. It'll be hard enough walking around without her parents there to justify her existence. It's happened before, the "Aha, that explains it" look that flickers across some people's faces when they see Ana with her family. Add blond hair to the mix, and Ana'll be likely to end up in a zoo.

She'll probably see that same look on Jamie's dad's face tonight. She can't imagine him fawning over her the way he did with Amanda. "Well, if all your friends are as *charming* and *blond* as this one! . . ." Ana smirks.

On the front of the package, the pale Asian girl looks blankly off into the distance, a shiny cap of bone-straight, honey-colored hair making her look like an exotic mannequin. Ana stands up and looks at herself in the mirror. Her toffee-brown-skinned reflection stares back at her with its almond eyes and frazzled brown curls. Not exactly starting out with the same equipment. It goes beyond skin color and hair type. The model has single-lidded eyes, like Ana's dad's, with one smooth lid that ends at the eyelash line. Ana is double-lidded, like her mother's family. Chelsea freaked out when Ana pointed it out one day.

"You know, this crease here"—Ana opened and closed her eyes a few times so Chelsea would see the fold she was talking about—"where beauty magazines tell you to put the second shade of eye shadow." She ran her finger across the crease. "Some Asian girls will actually have plastic surgery to fold the skin there and make their eyes look rounder and more European. It's called ble-pharoplasty."

"More like barf-a-row-plasty. That's gross," Chelsea said. Then again, Chelsea never wanted to look like anything other than a slightly taller version of herself.

What would Chelsea think about this? Or Ana's mom, for that matter? After years of straightening her hair, Ana's mom went all natural right before Sammy was born. "Black women have been trying to change who they are from the outside for far too long," she explained. "But it turns out, all hair is good hair. And being bald's fine too."

Ana laughed at the time. She was eight and the image of her mother with a shaved head was a weird one. Ana's mom went for twists instead, and occasionally braids. Ana's hair was straighter than her mom's, and she liked the curls it made. Sometimes. When her head wasn't damp and frizzy.

Ana hesitates. She promised her mom she'd be down soon. Besides which, Sunset Gold™ is an awful lot like "Mandy" Conrad's natural color. Does she really want to look like Amanda Conrad?

"She's such a cow," Ana reminds herself. With a sigh, she shoves the hair dye to the back of the cabinet under the sink. There's a really good chance she'd just end up looking like a clown anyway.

"So much for that." She fluffs her hair in the mirror and then pulls the ends tight, trying to smooth it down. "Yep. So much for that."

Instead, she steps into the shower and transforms into a nonblond but much cleaner Ana Mei Shen.

She pulls on her shorts and shirt and runs back downstairs to start Jamie's perfect dumplings.

8

The kitchen is a madhouse. Ana's mom has the hand mixer going on her cake, and her dad is halfway inside the refrigerator digging through the groceries. Grandma White is banging around in the cupboard under the stove where the pots are kept, and at the counter, Nai Nai is throwing handfuls of pork into a bowl while Sammy watches. All the noise together sounds like a bad elementary school marching band.

"Hey, honey," her mom says above the high whir of the mixer.

"Hey. Where's my pork?" Ana asks as she enters.

"Don't worry, Miss Impatient. It's right here." Nai Nai points to a butcher's parcel on the counter. "Now, pay attention, Sammy. There is a rhythm to this," she goes on. "If you do it right, the lion's head will be tender. Wrong . . . and you make a mess." She chuckles and scoops a handful of ground pork and tosses it against the bottom of the bowl with a light underhand maneuver that blends in the diced water chestnuts and soy sauce perfectly. Ana stands in the doorway and braces herself. Nai Nai's skill is just another reminder of how perfect her own dumplings will have to be. She takes two bowls from a cupboard.

Sammy stands on tiptoe to watch Nai Nai work. "Can I try it?"

"No."

"Please?"

"No." Nai Nai looks over her shoulder at Ana. "An-ah, your father will make the filling. Danny!"

Ana's dad pulls his head out of the refrigerator. "I'm still looking for the Chinese cabbage."

"Later. You help Ana. You start the dumpling filling. Ana will make the dough," Nai Nai announces.

"Nai Nai, *I'm* making the dumplings," Ana protests.

"No, you are too slow. You can stuff them. We will help now."

Ana gives in and puts an apron on. Aprons are kind of silly, but the last time she made dumplings, she was so covered in flour by the end that she looked like a snowman.

"Okay, this is going into the oven for half an hour," Ana's mom says, pouring her batter into a large sheet pan. "Watch it for me, and try to keep it down so it doesn't fall."

"What, baby?" Grandma White hollers, voice echoing in the cabinet she's rummaging through. "Where is my gumbo pot?"

"Up here, Grandma." Ana drags a chair over to a higher set of cabinets and wrestles down the cast-iron Dutch oven.

"Mama, do you have to do that now?" Ana's mom asks. She looks from the cake to Grandma White and Sammy. "Why don't we take the Samoan outside to run some laps? Come on, Sammy. Let's leave the kitchen to the pros for now."

"I am a pro," Grandma White says indignantly. Sammy is instantly swinging on her arm like a monkey.

"If he was a battery, we'd never run out of energy," she says. "I guess the gumbo can wait half an hour or so. Let us know when you-all are done."

"Will do," Ana says. The door swings shut and the kitchen is suddenly quieter.

Ana sifts a few cups of flour into one of her bowls and stands at the kitchen table, slowly mixing in a thin stream of water, while her father and Nai Nai work in unison, chopping vegetables for the dumpling filling and cabbage for the lion's head. With the kitchen reduced to only three cooks, a sense of calm prevails. She begins to work the dough with her hands. The kneading and the rhythm of the knives are soothing, and the whirlwind in Ana's head slows down just a bit.

Ana's dad and Nai Nai are like pianists playing a duet, small cleavers flying up and down like the velvet-covered hammers of piano keys, striking at water chestnuts, bok choy, gingerroot and garlic cloves, reducing each to a fragrant, uniformly diced pile.

"When do I get that superpower?" Ana asks.

Her father laughs. "When you practice it as much as I have with Nai Nai standing over you."

"I told you we were faster," Nai Nai says. "And your father is a slow learner. You'll do much better. Make the dough, then I will show you."

Ana finishes her dough and leaves the bowl under a damp cloth to rest.

Nai Nai stands beside her and holds up her cleaver, the sharp edge wet with juice from the gingerroot she's slicing. "Hold your knife at an angle and cut away from your fingers." She chops once, slowly, and then moves into a blur too fast for Ana to follow.

"Do that again?" Ana asks.

Nai Nai sighs and turns the blade, cutting the coins of ginger into matchsticks.

"Now, you mince it." She hands the cleaver to Ana. Ana looks at her dad. *Right, that looks easy.* He shrugs and steps away from the counter.

"I was a lot younger than you when I got my first knife lesson, tiger," he says.

Ana fumbles with the cleaver. "Right, like Mozart. 'All the Shens learn to cook from birth,' you told me."

Her father grins. Nai Nai shakes her head. "Tell the truth, Daniel. A lie will make the food taste bad."

58

He winces. "Okay, Ma. But some of this I don't think you know."

Nai Nai stops chopping. "You are my son, Daniel. I know everything."

"Did you know I stole Dad's army sword?"

Nai Nai hesitates a moment too long. "Of course."

Ana laughs. "My poor dumplings. Doomed before they're even made."

Nai Nai bumps Ana with her shoulder. "I am an old woman. Sometimes I forget. Daniel, tell us again, so I can punish you properly."

"I must have been about five years old when I found it under your bed."

"Daniel! What were you doing down there? So dirty and dusty like that."

"Not in your house, Ma. It was clean as a hospital. I was just playing around and my feet hit something, so I turned around and found this box lying there almost as long as I was tall. Well, Dad was downstairs reading a book, and Ma, you were getting ready to make dinner. So I shut the door and pulled the box out.

"Now, Ana, I was a pretty quiet kid."

Nai Nai shrugs. "Not always, but yes."

"But I was terrified of being found out. It was clear Ma knew about the box—she spent more time cleaning the house than I did getting it dirty again. And I always thought we were weird because we didn't have dust bunnies like the other kids' houses did.

"So I dragged the box to the closet, that big walk-in thing you guys had at the old house, and I hid behind your clothes so you wouldn't see me if you came upstairs. I remember the box was covered in old green cloth that smelled like old books.

"So I open it, and inside is the giant sword. At least, it looked huge to me at the time. And it was all shiny and new looking, because Ye Ye polished it every month, he told me later. It was as long as my leg, and the handle of the sword was bronze. The face of the hilt was rough, covered in some kind of bumpy leather. Turns out that was stingray skin.

"So there I was, feeling like I was King Arthur or something." Ana's dad puts down his cleaver and wipes his hands on a kitchen towel.

"So I picked up the sword, climbed onto my parents' bed and swung it up over my head with both hands." He mimics the movement, heaving his arms over his head. Ana giggles. She can just see him, younger than Sammy, legs spread wide for balance, swinging a giant sword.

"And I took a big chunk out of the ceiling. I mean a *big* chunk. Cottage cheese and plaster all over the place. It scared the life out of me. I couldn't get the sword back in the box fast enough."

Nai Nai gasps. Ana bursts out laughing.

"You put it back all dusty and everything?" Ana asks.

Her dad nods. "I didn't care. I could hear my dad running up the stairs. I'm trying to sweep the plaster off the bed when he comes charging in. *'Zhen me gao de?'* You know? 'What the hell are you doing, Daniel?' "

Ana gasps, she's laughing so hard. "I can't even picture Ye Ye raising his voice. He must've been really pissed."

Ana's dad nods. Nai Nai shakes her head and busies herself covering the bowl of minced pork with plastic wrap.

Ana's dad leans back against the counter, eyes bright with the memory. "Anyway, he sees the box sticking out from under the bed and the gouge in the ceiling and puts it together.

"I'm still on the bed and I'm crying because, you're right, he's never yelled at me like that before. So I think I'm going to get a spanking or something terrible is going to happen and he sits down on the bed and opens the box. He pats the bed for me to join him and I sit there, all snot-nosed and blubbery, as he examines the blade for nicks.

"And all he says to me is 'There is a proper way to treat a blade,' and shows me how to polish it.

"And when he's done, he looks up at the ceiling, smiles and says, 'Huh. Still sharp.' Not a single ding.

"So I start asking questions and he explained why the sword was so important, how he earned it as an officer in the Taiwanese Army in World War Two and he wore it in a big parade.

"I couldn't understand why he didn't show it off to everyone, but he said, 'That time is past, Daniel. I would rather think of the future, not the past.'

"Then he slides the box under the bed again. He

knows I won't mess with it a second time. And he says, 'Speaking of the future, it's time you learn something about knives. We can help your mother with supper.' And that's the day I had my first knife lesson."

Nai Nai wipes the last of the lion's head filling from her fingers, the perfectly shaped meatballs lined up in a glass dish in front of her. She turns to face Ana's dad. "Your father." She shakes her head.

"Really, Ma? You didn't know?" Ana's dad asks.

"I wondered, what's all this interest in cooking all of a sudden? But it didn't last. You helped me with two, three dinners, then I had to chase you down to get the same help."

"But wasn't there a big crack in the ceiling?" Ana asks. *Ye Ye must have been an old softy back then,* Ana thinks. He'd never let *her* get away with something like that.

Nai Nai shrugs and washes her hands. "We live in California. I thought it was from earthquakes."

Ana laughs. The lion's head is on the stove. The dumpling dough is resting. Her shoulders relax. She smiles. "This is kind of nice."

Her dad nods. "See, honey? We can be civilized sometimes. Right, Ma?"

Nai Nai nods. "I always say we should spend more time together." She dries her hands on a kitchen towel.

"Now, enough of this, it's time to cook. Ana, your filling is in the refrigerator. Your dough needs to rest. You can go back to the car. I forgot the rice."

"Okay." Ana washes her hands and takes off her apron.

"And get Mrs. White. It's time to start the gumbo."

"Okay." Ana starts to push open the door.

"Wait. No. I'll get the rice. You get Mrs. White. And where are you going, mister?" Nai Nai asks Ana's dad.

He pauses, head halfway out the back door. "I've got to set up the tables out back."

Nai Nai points a manicured finger at him. "Okay, but do not forget, you have the *lu bo gao* to do. I will not forget."

"Yes, ma'am," Ana's dad says with a sharp salute. He nods at Ana. "Miss Mississippi River Cruise," he says.

Ana smiles. "That's Miz Mississippi River Cruise to you, mister."

Her dad winks and slips out the door.

Nai Nai is going furiously through her purse. "Ana, we made a little mistake earlier with the *huen bao*."

"What?" Ana pats her back pocket. The small envelope is still there.

Her grandmother smiles, a weird, embarrassed little smile. Ana raises an eyebrow. "A simple mistake, really," Nai Nai says. "Ye Ye did not put everything inside like I asked." She closes her purse and thrusts a wad of tightly folded money into Ana's hand.

"It's nothing. Not a big-time river cruise. Just a little token. But we want you to have it." She pats Ana's cheek. "We are so very proud."

Ana blushes. *Note to self,* she thinks, *no more talking*

about the riverboat cruise. "Thanks, Nai Nai. It's really wonderful of you."

"Okay, silly girl, no time for sentimentality." Nai Nai waves away Ana's attempt at a hug. "We have dinner to make. I'll get the rice."

Ana takes a deep breath. "And I'll get the people."

9

"Ma, Grandma, the kitchen's yours," Ana calls, walking down the hallway. The house is as calm as she feels. Maybe the fourth time making a family dinner really is the charm. She checks the living room. Ye Ye is dozing in front of the television.

"Ye Ye, have you seen Ma and Grandma?"

He startles at her voice and shakes his head.

"Thanks." *Great.* Dinner is in a little more than two hours, and all the cooks have deserted. She runs upstairs and stuffs the *huen bao* into her nightstand drawer. She'll give it to her parents later, and they'll put it in her college savings account, no doubt.

She runs downstairs again and checks the backyard. The Shens' yard is a big empty space, towered over by two sycamore trees that drop their hard, bristly seedpods down on the family every summer. Ana and the Samoan used to take turns throwing them at each other, a Southern California version of a snowball fight.

The folding chairs for tonight's dinner are leaning up against the fence that borders the street. Sammy and her dad are struggling to set up the tables.

"Hey, sport," her dad says.

"Have you guys seen Mom or Grandma White?"

They shake their heads.

At the back of the yard, the garage door is open. Ana can hear the fryer going full speed. What she wouldn't do for a piece of chicken!

"Grandpa, are Mom and Grandma with you?" she shouts.

"Nope," he calls back.

"Chicken ready?"

"Great art takes time, grasshopper. You should've had that sandwich like your father asked."

"I didn't think I was hungry until I smelled the chicken," Ana says.

"Well, then, I'll be sure to let you all know when it's done."

" 'Kay. Thanks." Ana goes back inside.

"Ma? Grandma?" she calls.

Nai Nai is coming down the front hallway in a funny little crouch, a huge plastic bag of rice in her arms. "This

66

stupid bag," she says to Ana. "This is not my rice. And why is it plastic, anyway? This sharp rice pokes right through." She waddles toward Ana and the kitchen door. "Don't stand there, get the door—" Before she finishes the sentence, the kitchen door flies open and Grandma White strides out, holding a bag of jasmine rice between two fingers.

"Helen, baby, this ain't my rice."

Bam!

Ana winces. *If one grandmother leaves station A traveling at five miles per hour, and a second grandmother leaves station B traveling at seven miles per hour, who blames whom for the collision?*

"*Aiyo!*" Nai Nai screams.

"Lord have mercy!" Grandma White shouts.

"Oh, crap," Ana says out loud.

The hallway turns into a shaken snow globe, white grains of rice flying though the air and showering down over everyone.

"My head!" shouts Nai Nai, clutching her right eyebrow.

"Mm, mm, mm." Grandma White shakes her head and gives her chin a rub. "I think I fractured a denture."

Ana runs toward them. "Are you okay?" She grabs their hands.

"No, we are not okay. But you are okay. You are plenty okay. Go get me some ice," Nai Nai shouts, waving Ana away.

Ana gives up and turns to her other grandmother.

"Get me some ice too, honey. I swear this woman's trying to kill me."

"How can I kill you? You are like a big ox compared to me."

"What did you call me?"

"Nothing. I said you are *like* a big ox. Like. It's a smilie."

Ana tries not to laugh. *A smilie? Really?* She rushes into the kitchen, taking the time to prop the swinging door wide open. She scoops two handfuls of ice cubes into a couple of kitchen towels and takes them to her grandmothers, who have both found their way to the kitchen table.

"Are you guys okay? Can I get you anything?" Ana hates herself for wanting to laugh, because it really must have hurt. But the vision of her two locomotive grandmas colliding keeps replaying itself in her mind like an award-winning funny home video. She stifles a laugh.

The kitchen door swings open and Ye Ye enters at a slow and steady shuffle. Ana looks up to see him straddling the spilled rice in the open doorway. "What happened?"

Ana blushes involuntarily. It's not like it's her fault, but if it actually got Ye Ye's attention, it feels like a bad thing.

"Just a little accident," she says.

"No accident," Nai Nai complains. Suddenly, she waves her towel of ice in the air. "Sabotage. Yuan, they spilled my rice everywhere and tried to take my head off too. It's no wonder we can never have a nice meal at home with our own granddaughter. No wonder at all."

"Just a minute now," Grandma White says, one hand still clutching ice to her face. "Nothing here was intentional. You simply didn't watch where you were going and we ran into each other. Simple as that."

"Yeah, Ye Ye. Just an accident." Ana stands up, wondering if she should have held her tongue. Her grandfather regards her without expression.

"You will clean it up, Ana," he says finally. He turns to Nai Nai and says something in a stream of Chinese too fast for Ana to follow. She glances at her other grandmother, but Grandma White has her head down, concentrating on her ice. Ana shakes her head.

"What are you waiting for?" Ye Ye jabs a finger toward the hallway. He pats Nai Nai on the shoulder and shuffles back to wherever it was he came from. Ana shakes her head. *Thanks a lot, old man.*

"Go on, baby," Grandma White says.

"Okay," Ana says with a sigh. "Sorry." She's really starting to laugh. "I'll get the vacuum."

"No, no vacuum!" Grandma White exclaims. "That's good rice out there. Good rice. I brought it from Louisiana. You just pick that up and put it in a bowl."

Nai Nai nods her ice-packed head. "Yes, a bowl. For mine, too. That is high-quality jasmine rice. Excellent for cooking. Do not waste a single grain."

Ana stops laughing. "What? Are you serious?"

"Don't get sassy, baby," Grandma White says. "I hurt right now. Just do as we say."

"Grandma! Rice is rice. Plain and simple. Look at you, you've got half a bag."

69

Her grandmother eyes her steadily. "Do not argue with me, Miss Ana. Get that rice off the floor and back in the bag where it belongs."

Ana keeps her mouth shut. Her head is starting to hurt, and she didn't have to butt heads for it to happen.

She grabs the broom and dustpan from the pantry.

"Don't use that dirty thing on my food," Nai Nai says.

"Fine," Ana says exasperatedly. "God," she mutters to herself. She grabs two bowls and stomps back into the hallway. "Like we've got all afternoon."

"Ana."

It's Ye Ye, just around the corner in the living room, waving her over. She stifles a sigh.

"Yes, Ye Ye?"

His eyes stay on the TV, the volume low, but he waves Ana closer. "Ana, your grandmother is working very hard for you today. I do not like to see you be ungrateful."

Ana leans back.

She thinks of the giant check in her nightstand and feels her face grow hot. "I'm not ungrateful."

Her grandfather looks at her and Ana feels herself shrink about five inches. He grabs her by the wrist. Ana gasps in surprise.

"She asks for your help, you give it to her. Do not think you are smarter or better than your elders."

"I don't, Ye Ye, honestly. I'm picking up the rice right now." She hates the sound of her voice, like a whining little kid's.

Ye Ye looks at her a moment longer, then lets her go.

"Good." He settles back and turns up the volume a notch on the television.

Great. She goes back to the hallway, her proverbial tail between her legs. This is the man who let her dad get away with shoving a sword into the ceiling.

Un-freaking-believable.

She glances at her watch. It's almost five o'clock and she's on the floor picking up rice. So much for a charmed dinner. She lets her arms and neck go limp in exasperation.

"Man, I hate my life."

10

"How is everybody?" Ana sings as she breezes back into the kitchen with both bowls. If they don't look too closely, her grandmothers won't know that she fudged the job until they're already eating. Jasmine rice has a nuttier taste she just can't hide.

"That was easier than I thought," she says with the slightest prickle of guilt. Fortunately for Ana, Grandma White and Nai Nai have other things on their minds.

The kitchen has a distinct chill. Apparently, Nai Nai has gotten over her injuries. She is pulling the rice cooker out of the pantry. The big white and silver electric pot is almost as big as she is. Grandma White is still sitting at the table, looking forlornly off into space.

"Here, Nai Nai." Ana hurries to take the rice cooker from her grandmother. "I'll make the rice. You just rest."

"Good girl," Nai Nai says. "Finally, you are respecting your elders."

Ana forces a smile and dumps the mixed rice into the cooker. She does a quick search for any stray carpet fuzz before adding water and plugging in the rice cooker. Of course, they'll find out at dinner, but who knows? With Jamie's folks at the table, maybe nobody will say anything.

"There, all done. Now, anything else before I start the dumplings?"

"Watch the rice," Nai Nai says.

"Yes, ma'am."

Grandma White rises slowly and takes a glass from a cabinet. "I'm coming toward you now, so watch out," she says to Nai Nai. Gingerly, she works her way around Nai Nai, who simply shakes her head. Ana hears the ice cubes clunk into the sink and watches her grandmothers, one tall and brown, one small and pale, washing their hands.

"Ana, don't forget the lion's head, either," Nai Nai says, pointing at the pot of grapefruit-sized meatballs. "Cover it when it boils, then leave it alone."

"Okay," Ana agrees.

Nai Nai leaves and Grandma White breathes a little easier. Ana does too. Ye Ye's lecture still rankles a bit. Grandpa and Grandma White never make her feel so small.

"Baby, bring me some aspirin." Grandma White is holding her jaw where Nai Nai clocked her.

"Go sit down. I'll get it." Ana ducks out to the downstairs bathroom and brings back the bottle. Her mom still hasn't shown up.

"How's that?" Ana asks after Grandma White takes her aspirin.

"Baby, that woman has the hardest head on the planet. Am I bruising?" She holds her chin up to the light. Ana looks down at her grandmother and kisses her on the forehead.

"Barely a bump, Grandma." In a lower voice, she adds, "If she'd meant to hurt you, you'd be dead by now." Ana and her grandmother share a smile.

"That woman!" Grandma White exclaims. "If I didn't know better, I'd say she's got something against long-grain rice."

"No, just rice that doesn't stick together. Useless with chopsticks. And jasmine's got a different taste."

"I understand," Grandma White says. "Now to get this gumbo started," she adds, and rises slowly from the table. "All right now, Ana, help me with these shrimp." She pulls a bowl of unshelled shrimp from the refrigerator. Ana rolls up her sleeves and grabs a second bowl from the cabinet.

"Peel 'em and clean 'em for me." Grandma White gives her a knife for deveining each little gray shellfish. Ana may not have learned to handle a knife from Nai Nai, but Grandma White has certainly given her plenty of kitchen skills in the "clean this" department. From peeling shrimp to snapping the tough parts off green beans and shelling peas, Ana is a world-class menial laborer when she goes to visit her grandparents in Louisiana.

The vein is the grossest part, Ana thinks. *And not really a vein, either.* She stops thinking about it and gets to work, snapping off the legs and slipping the shrimp out of their shells like jackets.

"Do you just throw that away?" Nai Nai asks. Ana's skin tingles with surprise. Nai Nai is standing in the doorway, watching.

"Yep," Ana says.

Nai Nai clucks her tongue. "You could make a broth with that. Some good broth, too. Save me the shells. I'll show you. Do not waste food."

"It's not a waste, it's garbage." Grandma White turns around from the chopping board where she's been dicing celery. Ana smells the faintly salted, watery scent of the greens hanging in the air. "You throw it away. I know how to stretch a dollar, but that's not the way to do it."

Dear God, no, Ana prays silently. Her head throbs and she wishes she had taken some of Grandma White's aspirin. *Please don't let them get into a fight,* she thinks.

"Did you need something, Nai Nai?"

"Water," Nai Nai says quickly, and turns back to Grandma White. "You say you know, but it is wasteful," she insists. "I could make ten dishes out of everything you throw away today. Look at that celery. The leaves, what are you going to do with them?"

"Dice them up and use them as seasoning," Grandma White says.

Nai Nai frowns. "Oh, you just say that now. Now that you know I'm watching you."

"Here's your water," Ana says quickly, holding out a hastily filled glass. But the grandmothers aren't listening to her.

"No, I'm saying that because that's what I'm going to do," Grandma White says in her I'll-be-patient-but-barely teacher voice. "We all cook differently, Mei, but that doesn't make it wrong."

"The only thing I say is wrong is being wasteful. What's burning?"

"What?" Ana asks. She looks around the room. "Burning . . . ?"

Then she smells it.

"The cake! Oh, crap, the cake!" She grabs a pair of potholders and runs toward the oven, but it's too late. The cake comes out of the oven black on top and sunken in the middle. "How can that even happen?"

"Oh no, baby," Grandma White says, waving the smoke away. "Shut that oven door and turn on the vent."

"Take it outside," Nai Nai says. "You can scrape the top when it's cooled down."

"Scrape the top!" Ana exclaims. "It's a brick. A black brick. We can't serve this!"

She stomps outside, smoking cake pan in hand, and drops it on the flagstones in the backyard.

"My cake!"

Ana's mother comes running across the yard from the garage, a bucket of ice cream in her hands.

Ana's shoulders drop. "Sorry. I lost track of it."

"Oh." Her mom stares at the cake.

"Mom, where were you?"

"Sammy and I ran to the store for ice cream," Ana's mother explains. "I told Ye Ye."

"Open this door, get this smoke out," Nai Nai insists, shoving the door into Ana's back. Ana lets out an exasperated sigh, props open the door and follows her mother back inside.

Grandma White waves the rest of the smoke out of the kitchen with a dish towel. Ana's mom opens the freezer and tries to find a spot for the ice cream.

"Don't waste that cake," Nai Nai says again. "You can cover it up with that ice cream."

"Nai Nai, please," Ana says. "We've got people coming over in less than two hours and nothing is ready. The war is over. We've got plenty of food. Who cares if we throw away a burnt cake and some shrimp shells?" The minute the words are out of her mouth, she regrets it. *Great. Here comes the corn story.* Grandpa White's stories are always better than Nai Nai's.

Ana braces herself. Her mother rolls her eyes and deliberately hides behind the freezer door.

"Who cares? Who cares? Do you hear this one, Mrs. White? I will tell you who cares, Miss Ana 'I eat too much' Shen. *Starving* people care." Ana winces. "When Ye Ye was a little boy in China, he had to eat moldy corn, moldy corn in the fields because of what the Japanese army did to the crops, burning and taking everything. Do you understand? And he was lucky they didn't burn the fields, but left so much food to be gleaned. Or else he would have starved to death and you would not be here now. So do not ask me what is the big deal. The deal is very big. Very big indeed."

"Huh. Moldy corn," Grandma White says. She neatly folds the dish towel and starts chopping onions for the gumbo. Ana marvels at how onions never make her grandmother cry.

"That is right. Moldy corn." Nai Nai nods, satisfied.

"It's a wonder he even likes my corn bread," Grandma White says. Nai Nai frowns.

"He is just being polite." She grabs her glass of water from Ana and leaves the kitchen.

From behind the freezer door, Ana's mother starts to laugh.

"Don't laugh, now, Helen. Ana's granddaddy could tell the same story, but it's white beans. Navy beans. Ate so many of them when he was little that you'd think he had *joined* the navy. That's how his mother made ends meet during the Depression, and he hates them. Hates them to this day."

"We know, Mama," Ana's mother says.

Ana stays quiet. Her head is starting to really pound and there's a little muscle jumping over her right eye. She's heard the moldy corn story before, and the navy bean story, too. If she hears them again, she will scream. Time for a deep breath and polite conversation, she decides.

"Anything I can help with?"

"Aww, thank you, baby. Bring me those shrimp and get started chopping that sausage."

"Yes, ma'am."

Ana watches her grandmother begin the roux for the gumbo, dissolving flour in an equal amount of oil at the bottom of a big black Dutch oven, identical to one in Grandma White's house in Louisiana. Ana's mother wasn't allowed to leave home without a pot like that. One day, Ana will get one too.

"Now, close your eyes while I work my magic," Ana's grandmother says.

"That's not fair. I just saw you make the whole thing."

"Not all of it," Grandma White insists. "I still have my secrets."

"What. Ever," Ana whispers to herself, and turns her back to her grandmother. At least dinner is getting started.

"Aside from my beautiful cake," Ana's mom asks with a wry smile, "how's it going in here?"

"All right," Grandma White says. "We had a bit of a rice accident, and I'll have a lump in the morning, but it's fine right now."

"Rice accident? Do I even want to know what that means?"

"No," Ana says. "Just a spill."

"Just a spill?" Grandma White says indignantly. "More like an act of violence followed by an act of stupidity, and a whole lot of busywork."

Ana smirks and turns back around. "Yeah, well. It's over now."

"Uh-hmm." Grandma White turns the soup down and

pours herself a glass of water from the refrigerator pitcher. Ana's mom dances out of the way, frozen pork chops in either hand.

"Mama, will you cook these, too? We've got no room in the fridge."

"Ah, baby, now, you know we've got enough food for today. And they're frozen, besides."

Ana's mom does something she only does in front of Grandma and Grandpa White. She pouts. Ana can never believe it, no matter how many times she sees it. It's exactly the sort of response that she'd get in trouble for.

"I just don't want to take these back to the garage. I'm tired. I just want to sit down and make this stupid cake again."

"Mom, we don't need a cake," Ana starts to say, but Grandma White cuts her off.

"Are you whining?" Ana's grandmother asks. "Because if you're whining, I've got plenty of work for you to do. This is your daughter's day, and that cake better not be stupid. It better be as smart as my grandbaby is. And you should be grateful you've found a way to get everybody else to do the cooking. We've got people coming over tonight and they want to see a happy, smiling Helen, not some old grumpy thing. Isn't that right, Ana?"

"Yes, ma'am," Ana says brightly. She tries not to laugh as her mother scowls. At least the attention is off her for now.

"Fine, I'm not whining," Ana's mom says. "I'm not complaining at all." She drops into a chair and goes limp.

Ana laughs. "Here, Mom, I'll put the pork chops in the garage."

Ana pushes through the door just as Nai Nai comes the other way.

"What are you trying to do, kill me all over again?" Nai Nai hollers. "Oh, it's you, Ana. I thought it was your crazy grandmother with her bowls of cheap rice."

"Nai Nai!" Ana exclaims.

"What did you say?" Grandma White demands, a tea bag shaking in her hand.

"Hey, now." Ana's mom holds up her hands.

Ana's headache resurfaces. She clutches her pork chops and runs.

11

In the garage, Grandpa White is perched on an overturned bucket, putting the last of his battered chicken into a giant turkey fryer. The door is up, revealing his little campsite and a host of Ana's dad's tools. Besides being an architect, Ana's dad fancies himself a carpenter. He built the Samoan's tree house last year. Ana wishes he'd built one for her when she was Sammy's age.

"What's up, sweet pea?" Grandpa White asks when she enters. Ana shakes her head, but she can still hear the arguing going on inside.

"If Grandma and Nai Nai don't stop bickering, we'll never have anything for dinner." She walks past the workbenches to the big white freezer chest in the back of the garage and puts the pork chops inside. "Just this once, why can't everyone behave?"

Grandpa White shakes his head. He looks awfully serious for a man wearing a BOSS OF THE SAUCE apron. "Those women wouldn't know what to do if they couldn't argue. Why did God give them tongues?" He raises his eyes to heaven wearily. Ana drops her head to the top of the freezer, resting her cheek against the cool white metal with a sigh.

"It's worse than that, you know? It's like watching Chelsea's parents when they used to fight. Like little family earthquakes. Maybe one day everything will just shake apart." She looks down at the scratched surface of the freezer, her eyes stinging just a tiny bit. "What is with this family? Nobody likes anybody else. You all just pretend to."

Grandpa White shrugs. "I like them just as far as they like me. And you."

"Well, it sucks for dinner parties. Sometimes I think if Sammy and I weren't around, none of you guys would feel the need to get together and there'd be a little less fighting in the world."

Grandpa White looks at her, tongs balanced across one knee, fried chicken in the deep fryer in front of them bubbling away. Then he smiles.

"Baby girl, that's ridiculous." He shrugs and goes back to turning his chicken. "The two of you kids are our common ground, and that is a beautiful thing."

"That's me: Ana Shen, granddaughter, diplomat, peacemaker. Oh yeah, and salutatorian." *Sigh*. She stands up and paces across the garage.

Ana remembers the way Jamie Tabata's father looked down his nose at her. Obviously, he has someone more Amanda Conrad–like in mind for his son. Wouldn't that be great? If she and Jamie ever *did* date, Ana's not so sure she could deal with the parental garbage.

Grandpa White checks the thermometer on the fryer. "Well, cheer up, baby girl, 'cause things are just about to get a whole lot better." He smiles at her proudly. "Chicken's ready. You've never seen anyone fighting when they're eating fried chicken."

"Not sure that's a real test of the situation, Grandpa White."

"But it's true." He nods and picks up his tongs again. He drops the last drumstick in. The oil spatters, hot and snappy. Ana leans back, even though she's out of popping range. Grandpa White acts like he's made of asbestos. If he gets hit by the hot grease, it doesn't show.

"Want that drumstick?" he asks, pulling the first batch out of the fryer to rest on a plateful of paper towels.

"I don't think I can eat just yet. But I'll take a hug."

"Oh, well, those are ready to go too."

At least one grandfather likes her. Ana wraps her arms around him. Grandpa White smells like shoe polish and menthol. He likes to say the military taught him to shine his shoes until they look like glass and the AARP taught him to use mentholated cream to ease the pain of picking up the shoes. Ana kisses his cheek and then braces herself to go back inside. Less than two hours to go, and there's plenty left to do.

"Want something to drink? There's fresh iced tea."

"Let it get nice and cold first. I'll be in soon with the chicken."

"Okay. See you at the table."

The phone starts to ring the minute Ana enters the hallway.

"Telephoooooone!" Sammy screams out of nowhere. He explodes down the stairs and rushes past her through the kitchen door. Ana shakes her head.

"I'll get it," she shouts, but someone else picks up and the ringing stops. Ana sighs. What if it's Chelsea? Or worse, what if it's Jamie? Her heart skips a beat.

"Shush!" Ana's mother hisses. She's hovering nervously near the oven, a bowl of half-mixed white icing in her hands. "Don't you ruin this cake too." She turns the oven light on and peers through the window for telltale signs of a fallen middle.

"Sorry, Mom," Ana whispers. Grandma White bustles over to the stove. The hot sweet smell of baking cake mixes weirdly with the salty and tangy scent of Grandma White's gumbo.

Ana's mom shakes her head. She gives her icing a few more stirs. "Just don't shout, okay? Now, the timer's on, but if I don't hear it, just pull it out in twenty minutes. There's a cooling rack on the counter."

"Got it. I promise."

Ana's mom wraps the top of the icing bowl in plastic and kisses Ana on the cheek. "No tasting that. There's just enough to decorate the cake," she warns, and scurries off to another task.

On the stove, the broth for the lion's head is at a full boil. The smells of cabbage and pork float in the air. Ana's mouth waters.

"Whoops, I'm supposed to be watching this." She grabs a spoon and stirs the broth before covering the pot and lowering the flame. Fortunately, Nai Nai is on the phone.

"No, who are you? You were at the graduation today? Did you graduate? Good, good."

Ana cringes. Someone from school. She looks around. Her dad sits at the kitchen counter, cutting radishes into roses. He shrugs when she catches his eye.

"Hey, little bit." Grandpa White comes through the back kitchen door with a plate of fried chicken. He waves a piece in the air. "I did what I could."

Ana shrugs and joins him at the table. There's not enough room there for making dumplings, and Nai Nai is not giving up the phone anytime soon. Funny, but now that practically the whole family's in one place, she's got someone else she'd rather talk to.

"So, what is your GPA?" Nai Nai asks whoever is unlucky enough to be on the other end of the line in her ever-so-careful English. The way she says it, GPA sounds like a medical test rather than a grade-point average. "Not so good, but not too bad, either."

Oh God, Ana thinks. *Please don't be Jamie.*

"Derby," Grandma White says to Grandpa White, "I'm going to keep an eye on my gumbo." She gives a meaningful look at Nai Nai's back. Ana rolls her eyes. Even Nai Nai wouldn't stoop to sabotaging the soup. Apparently, Grandma White's not so sure. "Can you take Sammy out back to finish that little project I told you about?"

Grandpa White wipes some fried chicken crumbs from his mouth. "Come on, Sam. Your grandmother's got us painting again. Treats us like little kids," he says in mock indignation.

"I *am* a little kid, Grandpa." The Samoan grabs Grandpa White by the hand and tugs him out the back door.

Ana waits until they're gone, then sighs.

"How's it going?" her dad asks from his perch at the counter. Ana shakes her head.

"They'll be here in less than an hour. And I still have to do the dumplings, but I need the kitchen table. How about you? Where's our *lu bo gao*?"

He doesn't bat an eye. "I'm working on it."

"Right, Dad. I can see that. With little radish flowers."

"These are for your grandmother. My dish needs no decoration. Simple and perfect, that's my motto."

Ana smiles. "Since when?"

"Since I decided to make *mapo dofu* instead."

Ana laughs. *Lu bo gao* takes peeling and pounding at least a pound of turnip roots, but *mapo* is a stir fry—five to ten minutes of prep instead of five hours.

Ana's eyes drift back to Nai Nai, still on the phone.

"What about your parents?" she's asking. "What do they do?"

Whatever they do, Nai Nai approves. "Okay, Chelsea. Bye." She turns, nods at Ana and hangs up.

"Nai Nai!"

"Don't 'Nai Nai' me, now. I saw you forgot to turn down the lion's head. You want to eat good food, you have to help make it."

"Well, what did she want?"

"She can tell you later. Now you are washing your hands and making dumplings," Nai Nai says. "Then you can call your friend."

Nai Nai turns her attention to Ana's dad. "That Chelsea says her father is an engineer. A mechanical engineer. They make good money, very smart." She narrows her eyes at Ana's dad across the kitchen counter. "Such a shame. You should have stayed a structural engineer."

"Love you too, Mom," Ana's dad says.

"Love nothing. Love doesn't feed the family. Love only gets in the way."

Ana stops washing her hands long enough to look at her grandmother. "Nai Nai, why do you say things like that? You love Ye Ye."

"That's different. I'm smarter than both of you. I know how to fall in love with the right kind of man."

At the table, Grandma White harrumphs. Ana cuts her a warning look.

"I would ask what that's supposed to mean, but it's not worth it," Ana's dad says. "Here are your radish roses and your carrot flowers. Garnish away. I'm going to spend time with my wife. Whom I love. Very much." He winks at Grandma White, who smiles back, and he grabs a couple of drumsticks from Grandpa White's platter on the way out.

Ana turns to Grandma White. "Grandma, can you move your glass? I need the table for the dumplings."

"Sure, baby." Grandma White picks up her glass and folds her arms, watching over her gumbo like a pit bull. Ana's just glad there's no fighting going on. She wipes the table clean and spreads a couple of sheets of parchment paper on the table, Nai Nai's words ringing in her ears.

She can't help wondering if Jamie is the "right kind of man" for her, whatever that means. Nai Nai wouldn't think so, of course. Jamie is Japanese. For all Ana knows, he might be a direct descendant of the soldiers who burned those crops in China. He may as well have forced the moldy corn down Ye Ye's throat himself, as far as Nai Nai's probably concerned.

"Ana, don't forget your mother's cake this time. And don't touch the lion's head," Nai Nai says to Ana, looking at Grandma White. Nai Nai's eyes narrow slightly. "Just let it cook."

"Okay," Ana says, uncovering the bowl of dumpling dough.

"Okay." Nai Nai nods and pats Ana on the cheek. "You are such a good girl. We are so proud of you, aren't we, Mrs. White?"

89

Before Grandma White can answer, Nai Nai straightens her immaculate suit jacket and is gone.

"Thank goodness she's gone. We could all use some peace and quiet."

Ana moves around the table and kisses Grandma White's cheek. She can still smell the faint scent of onions and celery on her grandmother's skin.

"I'm sorry about Nai Nai. She can be so difficult sometimes."

"All the time," Grandma White says. "But that's not your fault, so don't apologize. We've been having our trouble since before you were born."

"I know." Ana sighs. "You'd just think it would be different after fifteen years." She ties her apron back on and gets the bowl of pork filling from the refrigerator.

Grandma White chuckles. "You'd think. But that's not the way things work. Shoot, you've got to realize there's a problem before you think about fixing it. And you have to know what the problem is. If it's just black versus Chinese, that's one thing, a thing that won't change. But there's something else about that woman. You know, she's never, ever called me by my first name? Always 'Mrs. White, Mrs. White, Mrs. White.' She likes your grandfather well enough, though."

"Yeah, I don't know what that's all about," Ana admits. "Dad says it's because she has a hard time saying *Olivia*. Maybe she's embarrassed?"

Grandma White stands up and goes to check on her gumbo pot. "Well, I guess I should be grateful that she calls me anything at all. When we first met, it was like we

90

weren't even at the same table. Like she'd frozen over solid or something. Now, Derby says it's my imagination. He could be right. Most times, our rivals don't even know our names."

"You guys aren't rivals," Ana says.

Grandma White cocks an eye at her. "Aren't we, though?"

Ana shrugs and pulls a piece of dough out of the bowl. "I guess. If you want to be America's Top Grandmother or something."

Grandma White laughs. "Maybe I do. Maybe I do." She stirs the gumbo pot and turns the flame down.

"Is that true?" Ana asks. "About rivals, I mean." She's pretty darn sure Amanda Conrad knows *her* name. But Grandma White nods.

"True as the nose on your face. There was a girl back when I was in high school, her name was Stella Reed. She thought she was the hottest thing since sunshine, and half the boys thought the same. Oh, how I hated her. Especially when she started dating my brother, your uncle Jacob. I couldn't understand how Jake could be so stupid. But he couldn't see through her. Put her up on a pedestal, like all the other boys did, and she kicked each and every one of them in the teeth.

"That was bad enough, but then she dumped my brother and went for the boy I had been seeing. And Timothy was a year younger than her, too! Can you imagine that?"

Ana's eyebrows go up into her hairline. "You dated?" She has a hard time imagining her grandmother dating in high school, let alone caught up in some kind of soap opera drama with the old-time equivalent of an Amanda Conrad.

Grandma White swats at her with a kitchen towel. "Yes, I dated. How do you think I met your grandfather? We weren't born old and married, Miss Smarty-pants."

Ana grins and dodges the towel. She starts patting the lump of dough in her hands into a flat disk.

"I ran into that Stella the other day at the hair salon," her grandmother says. "Seems she was in town for a convention. Selling makeup out the back of her truck. She looked it, too. No pedestals under her feet anymore. But even so, do you know she didn't recognize me? When I said, 'Hello, Stella,' she tried to sell me some reeking perfume. I had to tell her I was Jake's sister, and then remind her who Jake was. And I don't think she ever remembered Timothy, or what she did to him and me."

Ana can see it now. Amanda Conrad is probably somewhere flirting with some other boy, and Jamie Tabata doesn't matter to her one bit. That's a comforting thought. Unless, of course, it doesn't happen for another forty years, like it took for Stella Reed.

Grandma White snorts and washes off her tasting spoon. "And now, here I am still talking about her, when she's halfway to Tuscaloosa in her pink pickup truck with nothing but a gin and tonic on her mind."

"Grandma!" Ana feigns shock.

Grandma White smiles sheepishly. "Sorry, honey. I guess that old goat got to me. But that's my point in the end. This Jamie Tabata may be first in his class today, but September's a whole other story. Big fish in a small pond and all that. But you, baby girl, you've got the gills to keep on swimming. So don't be down. You'll do just fine."

"I guess." Ana sighs. She could use a life lesson right about now, but she's getting the wrong one. "The thing is, Grandma, I'm not sad that Jamie is valedictorian. It never really mattered to me. It's just that . . . well, you had Timothy, right?"

"Timothy? Timothy was a boyfriend, not a rival. He's—" Ana's grandmother stops in midsentence and the sun comes out in her eyes. "Oh! Oh, Ana dear, I had no idea. You're not competing with that boy, you're competing *for* him!"

Ana blushes. "I didn't think of it that way. But some of the other girls like him too. And now that we're going to high school, I guess I missed my chance."

"Now, now, the summer's just starting and he's not going to the moon, so you never know. But tell me one thing, sweetie." Grandma White gets serious. She wipes her hands on the kitchen towel draped across her shoulder and turns to face Ana head-on. "You are a bright, bright girl, and I'm proud of you, top, bottom or middle of your class. But tell me, did you let this Jamie person make valedictorian?"

"Let? What, like letting him win at tennis? No! Of course not. I didn't even know I was in the running until they announced it. Honestly, I didn't think I would be up there at all. Jamie's as smart as they say. *And* he's good at tennis. Well, table tennis, anyway." Ana smiles inside, remembering gym class with Jamie. They monopolized the table for three weeks, the Ping-Pong king and queen.

"Look at you." Grandma White shakes her head and clucks her tongue. "Uh-huh, there's a story there, in that smile," she says. "I'd like to hear it someday."

Ana blushes furiously.

"Don't worry, I can wait until it's less embarrassing," her grandmother says. "Of course, I'm going to have to pay extra attention to the young man tonight."

"Grandma!" Ana gasps.

Grandma White grins.

Just then, the oven timer goes off, *ding!* Ana jumps.

"That's Mom's cake. Can you put it on that rack?"

This time, the cake comes out golden brown and perfect.

"Well, that's one thing right today," Grandma White says. "That and my gumbo. Now, go on and call your friend Chelsea. I've got to check on your grandfather and Sammy."

"Right, Chelsea." Ana drops the first ball of dumpling dough back into the bowl. She wipes her hands and dials Chelsea's cell phone.

"This better be good news," she says.

It's not. Chelsea is going to be late.

12

Ana rubs flour on her hands and tries not to think about it. So what if her best friend/fashion advisor isn't coming early? She sprinkles a little flour on the parchment paper and tries not to think about it some more. Chelsea's coming late and Ana hasn't even started the pot stickers. Let alone picked out the perfect dress. Now she's got to do it without a second opinion. She sighs and looks at the clock. Not a lot of time, especially without Chelsea here to keep her sane, but she can still give it a go.

She starts making little balls of dough. Pork-filled pot stickers were the first Chinese dish she learned to make. Nai Nai would let her mix the dough, and Ana would watch her expertly stuff the dumplings, fat and crescent-shaped, like chunky little pieces of moon. Which is probably why Ana never quite got the hang of that step. That changes today. Today she will make perfect little purses of pork and ginger. Dumplings even Nai Nai would be proud to serve.

The dough is a warm off-white color and slightly sticky. It's relaxing to use her hands, after everything that's happened today. Good old-fashioned mindless cooking. No more freaking out about Jamie Tabata. No walking on eggshells trying to juggle the grandparents. Nothing but rolling balls of dough. The knot in her stomach disappears. It's pure bliss.

When the sheet of parchment paper is full, she presses each ball flat until it's the size of a drink coaster. Then she scoops out a tablespoonful of pork filling and drops one on each piece of dough. She picks up the first dough circle, cupping it in one hand and folding the dough like a taco around the meat. With the other hand, she pinches the outer edges together, sealing the meat in. It reminds her of the coil-and-pinch clay bowls she used to make with Grandma White when she was little.

Grandma White used to be an art teacher. When Ana was little, she loved to visit her grandparents in Louisiana and sit in on her grandmother's classes. None of Ana's friends had grandmothers with paint sets and easels or pottery wheels. Grandma White was the one who inspired Ana's mom to be an artist.

"We used to spend all our Sunday afternoons at the

museum," Ana's mom told her once. *The museum* meant the Art Institute in Chicago, where Ana's mom grew up. She said it the way other people called New York City *the city*, like there was only one in the whole wide world. To hear her mother talk about it, there might as well have been.

"Every week, after church, Daddy would go home, and it was just Mama and me. Those quiet white hallways, the staircase with the Chagall stained-glass window made me catch my breath every single time. Sometimes it felt holier than church."

Her mother had laughed at the memory that followed. "On the L ride home, I guess it was the graffiti on the walls that grabbed me. The fact that it was right out there for everyone to see. You didn't need to pay admission or wait for free Tuesdays. All you had to do was pass by on your way to school or work, even on your way to a funeral. Art for everyone. And that's why I'm a muralist."

Ana loves watching her mother work. The sides of the Los Angeles River basin and some of the underpasses on the 101 freeway toward downtown are smeared with colors her mother chose, and the faces of people, and landscapes that marry the Midwest with the South with the West and points beyond. Her favorite mural is of a cherry orchard, running along a stretch of the 110 before it reaches Chinatown. The pale pink blossoms look like strawberry ice cream on chocolate branches. Ana was eight the first time they drove past. It took three visits before she realized that among the painted people wandering beneath the painted trees were a younger version of her mother and father. They were holding hands, sitting under the smallest tree.

"That's a moment in time," Ana's mother told her. "That's when your dad proposed."

Ana's parents met when they were students, working on the same project in graduate school. Her father had designed a small gymnasium for a public park and Ana's mother was chosen to design a mural for one of the walls. It wasn't love at first sight, but according to her parents, it didn't take long.

Ana sighs and reaches for another ball of dough. It seems so obvious that her mom would become an artist, that her dad would fall in love with her. But here Ana is, starting high school in two and a half months, and there's not a single obvious thing in her future. It's like the rest of her family is carved out of something solid and strong, like iron or stone. Nai Nai will always be Nai Nai, her folks will always be Mom and Dad. Even Sammy will always be Sammy, no doubts there. But Ana . . . Her hand drops the ball of dough on the table, but she doesn't press it flat. Instead, she takes a deep breath.

"All things to all people," she tells herself. That's her job.

She presses her palm into the dough.

They all have love stories, too, including the Samoan. He has his stupid Girl Scout cookies that he adores beyond passion, and Nai Nai and Ye Ye have some odd, understated romance. She's only heard their story in bits and snatches here and there, but it feels exotic to Ana, the thought of marrying someone so much older than you and moving to a foreign country together. And Mom and Dad have their story painted under imaginary cherry trees on a dusty stretch of freeway. Grandma and Grandpa White have their love story, too, about meeting in a diner where Grandma baked pies after the Korean War. Yep, everyone has their love story, except for her.

Ana frowns. Jamie Tabata is coming over for dinner with his entire family. At least at the dance they could have been alone. He might even have kissed her. Her own backyard seems a far less likely setting.

A second later, the kitchen door opens. The peace and quiet was way too good to last.

"Oh, good, you can help me," her father says, coming through the door. Ana feels a twinge of guilt in her scalp. Her dad would flip if he knew she was daydreaming about some boy.

"Help you what, Dad? I'm elbow-deep in dumplings."

"Dumplings that I helped make the filling for, tiger," he reminds her, and rushes to the refrigerator. "I need you to chop and drain the tofu for me for the *mabo*."

Ana cuts him a look. "I've seen you work with a knife, Mr. Flying Fingers. That's going to take you all of ten seconds."

Her father straightens up and looks at her sternly. "You might be head of your class, but I'm head of this household."

Ana grins involuntarily. "Not today, you aren't. Or you wouldn't be sneaking around behind Nai Nai."

Her dad's shoulders drop. "I can chop stuff, it doesn't mean I can cook. And we've got"—he looks at his watch—"oh, under an hour. No room for error."

"Don't worry, Pops. I'll help you." She finishes the dumpling she's working on and moves to the sink to wash her hands. Her dad starts going through the pantry, pulling out cornstarch and Szechuan pepper, the hot spice with a strangely numbing effect on the tongue.

Ana opens the fridge and stares into the crammed shelves of leafy vegetables still sticking out of their grocery bags. "Where is Nai Nai, anyway? With Ye Ye? He's disappeared too."

"Don't think so," her dad says. "She was running to the store."

Ana eyes the refrigerator, packed to capacity and then some. She finds what she's looking for. "Really? What did we forget, spicy tofu? Pickled something or other?"

Ana's dad laughs. "I have no idea. She didn't say."

"Here's the green onions." Ana passes them to her dad for chopping. "At least she won't be answering the phone."

"Yeah. How did Chelsea take it?"

Ana shrugs. "Fine. She called to say they're going be a little late." She peels back the plastic cover on the first tub of tofu and pours the chalky water off the bean curd and into the sink. It swirls down the drain looking like halfhearted milk. Ana stares at the spongy brick of tofu left behind. Suddenly, it all seems hopeless. Making a meal out of a flavorless block of curd is like a magic trick. She looks up from the sink and over to where her dad is slicing green onions. The dumplings on the table are nowhere near done. She hasn't even had a real lunch today and her hair is still wet and twisted up into little-girl braids, not to mention the still-not-in-a-sundress problem and the "here's some cash to buy your love" incident with Nai Nai.

"This sucks."

"What sucks?"

"Well, maybe we should just order pizza. The rest of this stuff isn't really coming together."

Her father stops chopping. "You'd have a mutiny on your hands, honey. I haven't seen this big a joint effort since the Berlin Wall came down."

"Yeah, I guess." She sighs, a tired feeling creeping over her shoulders. *Maybe that's why I fell asleep in the car. Avoidance.* "It's just so much work, and anxiety."

"Anxiety?" Her dad wipes his hands on a kitchen towel. He comes over and puts an arm around her. "You want to tell me what's on your mind?"

Ana puts the tofu package down and rests the heels of her hands on the edge of the sink. "It's just . . . sometimes I feel like . . ." She pauses and gathers her thoughts. "You know when you were a kid, and Russia and the U.S. were all angry at each other?"

"The Cold War?" her dad asks with some surprise.

"Yeah, that. And you said you lived with the threat of nuclear war every day?" She turns to face him.

Her dad shrugs. "Well, not every day. Not consciously, but yeah, it was a different time."

Ana shakes her head. "Not so different anymore. But

the thing is, Dad, sometimes that's how it feels around here. Like there's all this tension all the time, and like I'm in the middle, like Switzerland or something. But I don't know which side I'm supposed to be on."

Her dad pats her shoulder and they both lean their backs up against the sink. "And it's not just at home, but at school, too, like I don't know who I'm supposed to be." Ana frowns. Mandy Conrad or Ana Shen? Ana Shen or Ana White Shen, like her mom? Or maybe even Ana White-Shen-Tabata. God, Mandy Conrad doesn't hyphenate and she probably wears a sundress all the time and has a personal chef to make the dumplings. *Ugh*. The stomach knots are back.

Her dad sighs and it sounds so sad, Ana wishes she hadn't said anything.

"Honey," he says, "your mother and I knew it might be hard for you and Sammy to grow up biracial. But it's not about taking sides. You are the best of both of us, the best we have to offer as human beings. Our cultural differences only enrich us and make us stronger."

Ana stares at her dad, her mouth opens but no words come out. He takes a deep breath and continues.

"You're growing up, tiger, and the world's not always going to be a friendly place. But look, it's like . . ." He looks around the room and sees the jar of Szechuan chilies. He holds it up to her.

"It's like Chinese cooking. All our differences are like different flavors. Some are hot like these chilies, or sour like vinegar, or salty like dried shrimp, or sweet like melon. They're all so different from each other, but take a bite of one of those dumplings dipped in vinegar and soy sauce, and it's delicious. Ana, it's perfect."

He cups her cheek in his free hand. He looks so earnest that Ana can't hide it anymore.

"Dad, I've got a total crush on Jamie Tabata and I'm, like, freaking out. This dinner has to be good."

Her dad freezes. She can feel the hand on her cheek stiffen.

"What?" he says slowly.

"Um . . ." Ana's mind starts racing. "Oh . . . oh! No, Dad, this isn't a race thing. I mean, I know who I am, sort of, that way. But I'm not a little kid anymore and you keep calling me tiger and everybody wants me to do what they want me to do, but today is supposed to be my day and I've got things I want to do. Like make perfect dumplings and have dinner with a boy. So I've got to finish cooking, and I've got to get dressed, because I don't want to look like a total disaster when he comes over. Sorry to freak you out. I know you said no boys until I'm twenty-one, but be realistic, it's happening. Well, maybe, it's at least starting, and I thought you should know."

Her dad blinks like he's moving in slow motion. His hand falls away from her face.

"Wow." He takes a step back and frowns at the floor. "Huh. Wow." He rubs his eyes. "Um . . . This kid, Jamie . . . Tabata?"

Ana's face goes hot, the embarrassment finally catching up with her mile-a-minute confession.

Her dad swallows. "Is he . . ."

"He's the valedictorian, Dad. He's smart, he doesn't do drugs or anything, and he's the same age as me."

Her father nods. "Right. Good. Good, just so we're clear." He nods a few more times. "All right. Can't wait to meet him."

Ana breathes a sigh of relief. "Thanks, Daddy."

She gives him a hug. He quirks an eyebrow at her.

"Don't you mean 'Dad'?"

Ana smiles. "Sometimes. And sometimes 'Daddy.' "

"So where's my tofu? You've got to get dressed and all," her dad says.

"Right." Ana pulls the tofu out of the package and places it on the chopping board.

"Hey, Dad? Where's Ye Ye?"

13

"Hey, guys," Ana's mom interrupts, coming in through the back door before Ana's dad can answer. "I thought I'd cut some mint for the iced tea," she explains.

She squeezes between them to drop the mint into the sink. She pulls off her gardening gloves.

"Have either of you seen my father?" she asks, turning on the water and rinsing the leaves. "Mama's looking for him."

"Like, half an hour ago," Ana says. She finishes cutting the tofu into cubes and passes the plate to her dad. "I was just asking about Ye Ye."

"I thought he was online in your dad's office." Ana's

mom shakes her head. "Well, as long as everyone shows up for dinner, I'll be happy. But it sure is nice and quiet with them gone."

Ana grins and goes back to her dumplings. "How many more of these should I make?"

Her parents survey her handiwork. "Let's see," her dad says. "Chelsea, her sister and dad . . . us . . . them . . . fourteen people. Figure three dumplings each . . . I'd say make twelve more and we're set. We've got a lot of food to spread around."

"Good." Ana tears off another sheet of parchment paper and rolls more balls of dough. She powers through the last dozen dumplings and pulls out a large frying pan.

"Dad, will you cook these?"

"Sure, tiger . . . Ana. Do you mind rounding everyone up? Then you can get ready."

"Sure thing." She washes her arms up to her elbows, dries them on a towel and dashes out the door.

"Grandma, Grandpa, Ye Ye, Nai Nai," she yells through the hallway. "Dinner's ready to go!"

She makes it to her dad's office on the first floor, where Ye Ye is nodding off at the desk in front of the computer.

"Have you been here this whole time?" Ana asks. Ye Ye shrugs. She's the only person in the world with cyberfriendly grandparents. Go figure.

"Well, they need you in the kitchen."

"I'm coming, I'm coming," he says, and rubs the sleep from his eyes.

Nai Nai comes rushing through the front door on Ana's way back. "An-ah, carry these bags in for me."

She shoves a shopping bag at Ana and hurries on to the kitchen. The bag is heavy enough to catch Ana by surprise. She looks inside. A watermelon and a box of frozen dumplings look back at her.

"Nai Nai," she calls, "I *made* the dumplings." She can even hear them sizzling away in the kitchen. Her grandmother sticks her head around the kitchen door.

"When I left you were just *talking* about making dumplings. This way we can be sure. Bring me that melon. Where is your grandfather? He can slice it."

"In the office. He's coming," Ana says. She carries the bag into the kitchen and puts it on the counter.

"See, Nai Nai." Ana points at the cooking dumplings. "In the pan and ready to go."

"Harrumph," is all Nai Nai says.

Ana shoves the bag of store-bought dumplings into the freezer. Even if hers are only half done, there's no way she's letting them be compared to these perfectly shaped things. "I didn't see Sammy and Grandma White," she tells her mom.

"They're out back. I just sent your dad out to help finish setting up," Ana's mom says. The sheet cake on the table is now iced with white frosting, plain as a field of snow.

Just then, Ye Ye shuffles through the doorway with a sheaf of papers in his hand. Ana steps aside to let him pass.

"Oh, good. Ye Ye can cut up the melon. Can I get dressed now?" Ana asks, trying not to sound like she's complaining.

"Yes, hurry up. Go." Her mom waves her away.

Grandma White passes her in the doorway with Sammy in tow. "Our little project is up and running," Grandma White says.

Ana shakes her head. "Geez, it's like rush hour in here."

"Oh, An-ah!" Nai Nai sings out. Ana stops in her tracks and sticks her head back through the swinging door.

"Yes?" she says as sweetly as she can. It's game time and everything is going . . . well, reasonably well. *Put on your patience hat,* she tells herself.

"Come here, granddaughter, there is something Ye Ye and I have been wanting to share with you."

Ana tries not to sigh or drag her feet when she goes back into the kitchen. Grandma White and Sammy are sitting at the table with Grandpa White; her parents are pulling out platters to hold dinner. Nai Nai has put her bags down and is standing with her back to the refrigerator. Everyone is listening.

"Granddaughter Ana. Your grandfather and I are so very proud of you on your graduation day that we've decided to do something a little earlier than we had planned."

Ana slowly steps forward. *This doesn't sound good,* she thinks. "But Nai Nai, you've been so generous already," she says. She glances around the room. Her parents are completely in the dark, from the look on their faces. Grandma White is raising an eyebrow. It makes her look more like a teacher than ever.

Nai Nai claps her hands sharply. "We are taking you to Taiwan!"

Ana's eyes go wide. "What? Really?"

"Show her, Yuan. First class all the way!"

Nai Nai pushes Ye Ye forward. He smiles gently and hands her a sheet of paper. Ana scans it.

"It's a boarding pass . . . and a hotel reservation." She flips through the pages. "Ye Ye, is this what you were doing online?"

Her grandfather chuckles. "It was your grandmother's idea."

"This is fantastic!" Ana says. "First class!"

Her father makes a strangled sound—a cheer interrupted by Ana's mother's foot on his toes.

Right, Ana thinks. She tries not to look at Grandma White. *Way to go, Ana.* "What a surprise," she says. "A last-minute surprise!" Her smile wobbles a little.

Nai Nai doesn't notice. She's too busy clapping her hands to punctuate her words. "It's not too last-minute. We planned this all along. I mean, we were going to wait until you graduated from high school, but kids are so different these days, you are old enough now. And besides, then you will have college to worry about, and we don't want to distract our salutatorian!" Nai Nai flutters forward, her hands waving in the air until they land on either side of Ana's face in a little affectionate squeeze. "Isn't that good news! A first-class trip to Taiwan!"

"That's fantastic, Nai Nai. Really." Ana smiles and gives her grandmother a hug. Over Nai Nai's shoulder, Ana sees her parents smile, but they don't relax.

"That's wonderful," Grandpa White says. Sammy giggles. "Isn't that wonderful, Olivia?"

Grandma White doesn't answer.

Ana takes a deep breath, disengages and rushes over to Grandma White's side. She gives her other grandmother a big hug and kiss. "A riverboat cruise—*mwah!*" She goes back to Nai Nai. "And a trip to Taiwan—*mwah! I really am the luckiest kid in the world."

"Yes, you are," Ana's mother agrees. Ana's parents squeeze hands. Ana is a diplomat and they know it. Everyone is smiling, except for Grandma White. The rest of Ana's family relaxes back into the flow of finishing dinner.

"Well, I should go get dressed now," Ana says, and starts to back away toward the door.

"Baby?" Grandma White waves her back and pulls her in to whisper in her ear. She slides an opal bracelet off her wrist.

"Here, wear this tonight for good luck."

Ana hesitates. *This is too weird.* "Uh . . . thanks." She accepts the bracelet.

No one else even notices, except for Nai Nai, who begins removing her earrings. "And these, too, Ana, for luck," she says pointedly.

"Um, Nai Nai, I don't have pierced ears," Ana says apologetically.

"Oh." Nai Nai mutters something under her breath in Mandarin. "Here." She struggles to remove a ring. It barely fits on Ana's pinky.

"Thanks, both of you. I'm going to go put these on right now."

Her grandmothers are not looking at her anymore, just at each other.

"Oh, and baby girl?" Grandma White says. "What your grandmother said earlier about worrying about college . . . Well, you don't have to. *We* weren't going to tell you until you graduated from high school, but your grandfather and I have been saving ever since you were born, ever since your mother met your father and we knew that they would have children. You and Sammy can both go to the college of your choice. Now, isn't that nice?"

Ana's mother drops a dish. Everyone turns to watch it bounce, but it doesn't shatter.

"You what, Mama?"

"You heard me, baby. Ana's college is paid for. At least it will be by the time she's eighteen."

"Oh, lord," Grandpa White says softly.

Ana's mother bursts into a grin. "That's . . . that's amazing. Daniel? That's amazing."

"Wow," Ana's dad says, and hugs Ana's mom.

Nai Nai has turned pale.

"We'll buy you a house," she says in a clipped voice. "You can have our house when we are dead."

Ana spins around. "What? That's just crazy. I'm only fourteen!"

"And we are healthy. It is just a little something for the future." Nai Nai sits back, satisfied. Ana, however, is not.

"I don't want your house!"

"It's not good enough?"

"No! It's yours!"

"Hmph!" Nai Nai folds her arms angrily.

"No, it's good, of course it's good, it's wonderful, but it's yours! I don't want you to die! I don't want to live in Irvine! I want . . . well, I don't know what I want, but I'm fourteen! I don't have to know just yet, do I? I don't know where I'm going to college, or where I want to live when I graduate, but that's eight years from now. Stop pushing me. Both of you!"

Her grandmothers sit back, hurt looks on their faces. Ana's parents' mouths open, but nothing comes out. Even Ye Ye is speechless. Ana cringes. It's like time has frozen, and it's about to hit the ground and shatter and she can't stop it. Her head spins as she reaches for the right thing to say, anything to get that look off her grandmothers' faces. Anything to keep from being the ungrateful little girl Ye Ye warned her about. The right words to keep everyone else happy, even if she's not.

Then the doorbell rings.

Everyone freezes. The silence in the kitchen stretches painfully.

The doorbell rings again.

Ana lets go of a breath she didn't know she was holding.

"I'll get it," she says quietly.

She unties her apron and stalks out of the kitchen to the front door. She throws the door open.

"Chelsea, you won't believe it—"

"Hi."

It's not Chelsea. Ana blinks in the sunlight.

"Jamie?"

He smiles at her nervously. "Uh . . . yeah. Hi. Are we early?"

12

"Hiiiiii," she says, the greeting falling out of her mouth like a dead leaf.

Jamie smiles. His dad and mom are standing behind him like that *American Gothic* painting of the farmer and his daughter with the pitchfork, only the pitchfork is Mr. Tabata's long finger digging into his son's shoulder.

"Miss Shen," Mr. Tabata says.

Ana feels short and dark in front of him. Then she realizes he's blocking the light. She steps out of his shadow and instantly regrets it. She knows how she must look, like a kid playing with Play-Doh. Her shirt is smeared with streaks of dough and dusted with flour. Even her shorts have seen better days.

"Um . . . Come on in." Briefly, she hopes Jamie's dad isn't a vampire or something. But there's enough garlic in dinner to kill a whole castle full of vampires.

Ana leads the way down the hall, her palms suddenly sweaty and the back of her neck itchy. Jamie Tabata is actually here, inside her house. It's weird. She feels like she's floating two inches outside her own body. Her T-shirt feels hot and her legs prickle with a sudden sheen of sweat. The angry knot in her stomach feels like a lead weight.

"Everyone's still in the kitchen dishing up the food. We're going to eat in the backyard."

Jamie's mother smiles. "How lovely," she says. It's the first thing Ana's heard her say all day.

"It's a nice evening," Jamie's father agrees, but it sounds more like small talk than pleasure.

The short walk past the closed kitchen door to the backyard feels like forever, like a march down death row in an old prison movie. Ana is more than happy to throw open the door to the yard. She resists the urge to run through it and jump the wall to freedom. Nothing is going the way she wanted it to, not a single thing.

A burst of cool air greets them, and a sight Ana was afraid she'd never see.

Grandma White has transformed the backyard into a paradise. Where there was once only patchy grass beneath the shedding eucalyptus trees, now there are fairy lights, tiny chains of brightness twinkling in the branches. And the sky is just edging toward purple, that moment that could be sunset or dawn and is full of softly colored promise. The two folding tables are set together to make one long one and covered with festive oilcloths, turquoise backgrounds dotted with a parade of red and orange fruits. A few tabletop paper lanterns light the table, set at intervals along the center, just wide enough apart to make room for the food.

"Wow," Jamie says.

"Hurray!" Sammy scampers out the back door and cheers when he sees Jamie's family. He points to the sign draped across the side of the garage. "Grandma and I made this."

WELCOME, GRADUATES, it reads in big red letters painted on the cleaner side of an old bedsheet. *Ah,* thinks Ana, *that was the special project*. Hard to believe it was done by the same grandmother who just drove her so crazy.

"How beautiful," Jamie's mother says.

Ana blushes. "Thanks. Um . . . have a seat. Can I get you something to drink?"

With orders for iced tea for Mr. and Mrs. Tabata, and lemonade for Jamie and Sammy, Ana returns to the house. She steps into the hallway rather than straight into the kitchen, unsure how to face her family. She's not wearing a sundress, and she's not exactly speaking to her relatives, but the backyard turned out perfect. She shakes her head and rubs her temples. It just doesn't make any sense.

The back door swings slowly open. Jamie sticks his head in. "Oh, Ana."

She starts, then pulls herself away from the wall. Her heart pounds unreasonably loudly.

"Hey, Jamie. Um, I was just about to . . ."

"Yeah, uh, I came to help with the drinks. Oh, and to give you this." He holds up a pink pastry box tied with a bit of string. "I wanted to make something, since everyone else was cooking. But my dad thought these would be better."

"Oh. Thanks. You didn't need to bring anything." Ana takes the box with only slightly trembling fingers and slides back the string to look inside. Little translucent pink- and green-frosted cubes with sugared flower petals on top sit on a sheet of wax paper. They look like something you'd serve at a tea party.

"They're whatchamacallits," Jamie says. "Petits fours. Like little cakes."

"Great. Thanks." She smiles and tries not to worry about serving them alongside her mom's giant sheet cake.

They stand there in the hallway staring at each other. Ana's heartbeat pounds even more loudly in her ears. Her face must be shaking, her heart's beating so hard.

"So," she says, and clears her throat. "Iced tea, right?"

"And lemonade."

The hallway that seemed so long a few minutes ago feels tiny now. Ana is close enough to Jamie to feel the heat coming off his body.

"Thanks for having us over, Ana. I'm really—"

Ding-dong! The doorbell chimes so unexpectedly that Ana almost drops the petits fours.

"Yikes. That's probably Chelsea," she explains. "I'll get it!" she calls out. She hands the pastry box back to Jamie and leads the way to the front of the house.

"Chelsea, thank God, I—" Ana stops in midgreeting.

Amanda Conrad is standing there, all five feet and seven inches of her, a breezy blue and green sundress billowing around her long legs and the sun setting like a freaking halo right behind her Honey Blonde™ hair.

"Amanda?" Ana stands there like a kid with a geometry problem she has to solve in front of the whole class.

"Hi, Ana. Jamie!" She squeals his name. "Surprise! Jamie's dad invited me. Isn't that great? Oh, this is my mom." She jabs a thumb at the woman standing by the sidewalk, finishing a cigarette. Mrs. Conrad is an older, tired-looking version of Amanda. She waves and stubs out her smoke on the sidewalk with an astonishingly high-heeled shoe. "Sorry. Nasty habit. Hi."

"Ooo, are those petits fours?" Amanda pushes her way past Ana and winds one of her long arms through Jamie's. "I adore petits fours!" she exclaims, dragging out the word *adore* in a way that makes Ana want to punch her in the stomach. And kill Jamie's dad.

"Congratulations, Hannah," Mrs. Conrad says.

"Ana," Ana corrects her.

Mrs. Conrad laughs. "Oh. Hannah's such a pretty name. So, this is the great Jamie Tabata."

She smiles charmingly. Ana bristles. Mandy and her mother are cut from the same golden California cloth, but

Mrs. Conrad's had some nipping and tucking to keep her edges from fraying.

"Hi, Mrs. Conrad." Jamie shakes her hand. Ana groans inwardly. Turns out the real vampires never ask to be let in. They just show up.

"We were just getting drinks," Jamie says.

"Ooo, I'd love a drink. What are you drinking, Jamie?"

"Lemonade."

"Oh. I'll have one too," Mrs. Conrad says to Ana. "I adore lemonade."

Ana tries to catch Jamie's eye, but the Conrad women are all over him.

"I'll take them outside." Jamie leads Amanda and her mom away, looking for all the world like a rock star with a groupie entourage.

Now Ana has no choice but to talk to her family again.

"I'll warn them in the kitchen," she mutters under her breath. Ana grits her teeth and stands in the doorway for a moment, trying to take a calming deep breath and failing. The sun is fading behind the trees.

"Dad, just take the tie off!"

Ana sighs with relief. It's Chelsea's voice, coming over the hedge that shields their front yard from the street. A second later, Chelsea herself appears, followed by her father, "Chuck"—who is fumbling with his tie, never mind the button that's popped open over his belly—and Dina, Chelsea's enthusiastic little sister.

"Ana!" Dina squeals, flashing braces.

"Hi, Dina."

Chelsea frowns. "Ana? You all right?"

Ana looks at her friend and feels a wave of nausea grip her stomach. "No. I hate my family. And Amanda Conrad's here."

15

"There's gonna be two more people for dinner."

Ana leans up against the kitchen doorjamb and hangs her head.

"Two? Two more?" Nai Nai repeats. Chelsea pats Ana's shoulder. Chelsea's family has followed the Conrads to the backyard. She's with Ana for emotional support.

"Hi, Mrs. Shen, Mrs. Shen, Mrs. White, everybody."

"Hi, Chelsea," Ana's mom says. "So, who else showed up?"

Ana looks up at her mother, grateful that the family drama is being ignored for the moment. "Amanda Conrad." She spits the name out. Grandma and Grandpa White exchange a questioning glance.

"Amanda Conrad . . . she's a good one, right?" Ana's dad asks. The soups are ready, the lion's head and gumbo dumped into giant bowls, with a smaller bowl of rice half filled on the counter. Looks like the dinner plans carried on without Ana.

"No! She's the bad one! She's the freaking goddess of all things annoying and bad."

Ana shakes her head. Family can be so stupid sometimes. They are loud, dense, sloppy and embarrassing, or just plain weird. They make themselves so obvious it's like there's a sign flashing over their heads that says AB-NORMAL. Ana grimaces. Tonight is going to suck.

"Amanda Conrad. That's the horsy one," Ana's mom says.

Ana snorts and relaxes a little. "See, Dad. Mom listens."

The room seems to take a deep breath. Ana still can't bring herself to look her grandparents in the eye, but she doesn't have to. Not yet, at least.

"I never did the *mapo*," Ana's dad says.

"That's okay, hon, the cake's not done either." Ana's mother surveys the kitchen. "Let's just pull together what we have. We can always come back for round two."

Trays are assembled. Faces are splashed with cold water.

"Didn't you want to put on a dress?" her dad asks.

Ana shrugs. "It's too late now."

Dishes clatter, pitchers are filled, and the Shen family moves into the backyard more or less en masse, a chocolate and caramel-colored army, armed with dinner.

General Ana Mei Shen rides at the head, resplendent in her battle-smeared polo shirt and shorts.

"Mom, Dad, you remember everybody."

Ana can't help noticing the look on Mr. Tabata's face when her parents come out. The old "Ah, that's what she is" face. Ana's jaw goes tight, but she smiles anyway.

"Of course." Ana's mom steps forward with the lemonade and iced tea and places both pitchers on the table. She reaches out a hand to Mr. Tabata and Mrs. Conrad. There is a general hubbub of hellos, and a clatter of platters meeting the table. The table falls into the following formation: Ana's parents sit at either end, with Sammy next to their dad and Ana sitting in the obvious place of honor at the center in a chair draped with crepe paper. Grandpa and Grandma White are on her left, Chelsea, Dina and Chelsea's dad on her right. Jamie is squeezed in between Amanda Conrad, who is right across from Ana, and Mr. T. Ana sighs. She should've put a tack on that seat.

Mrs. T is to the right, next to Ana's dad. Then, for some reason, Nai Nai and Ye Ye have squeezed in, putting Mrs. Conrad at the end, across from Chelsea's dad and next to Ana's mom.

"Oh, we forgot the glasses." Ana rises. Chelsea and Jamie pop up, but Chelsea is faster.

"I'll help." The two girls retreat to the kitchen.

"Holy crap," Chelsea says. "And she's sitting next to him too."

"Yeah. Surprise!" Ana throws her hands up in mock glee. "I knew it was too good to be true."

Chelsea pats her shoulder. "You poor thing."

"You don't even know. Like, right before Jamie showed up, I had a big blowup with my grandmothers. Huge."

"What, about the *huen bao*?"

"Yeah. And the first-class ticket to Taiwan they 'forgot' to give me. And my college tuition and a house. That's the going rate for granddaughters these days, I guess."

Chelsea gives a low whistle. "Geez. All I ever get is frozen yogurt." She looks to see if Ana will smile.

"Hardee-har-har. Yeah, it's funny now, but I'm surprised I haven't been grounded." Ana shakes her head and laughs in disbelief. "You know, I almost dyed my hair today."

Chelsea's eyes widen. "What? No way."

"Yep. Blond. Honey blonde, to be exact."

Silence.

Chelsea laughs. "You're not serious, are you?"

Ana pulls a stack of acrylic cups from a cabinet without answering.

"Wow. That's crazy." Chelsea scratches her cheek. "You know, I once ate brownies for a week because your granddad said it would make me brown like you."

"He did not."

"Yeah, he did. We were in first grade and I thought you were so pretty. I wanted to look like you."

Chelsea and Ana stare at each other for a long time.

"But I needed braces," Ana blurts out.

"So did I. Point being, you'd look dumb as a blond."

Ana makes a straight face. "Like Mandy Conrad."

They break into a laugh that lifts Ana's spirits enough to face the crowd outside . . . where there is more tension, courtesy of Nai Nai, who is saying to Mr. Tabata, "You look very Japanese."

Mr. Tabata blinks. Ana cringes. Chelsea snorts and they hold back from the table.

"Well, thank you," Mr. Tabata says slowly.

"My husband fought the Japanese," Nai Nai continues helpfully.

"Nai Nai, war isn't exactly an icebreaker," Ana says, coming forward to pass the cups around. Apparently, it is, because both of Ana's parents start to talk, offering to pour drinks for anyone who's interested.

Then Ye Ye clears his throat and speaks for what might be only the third time all day.

"I do not talk about the war," he announces clearly over everyone else's hurried mumblings.

"We know, Dad," Ana's father says. "So, that was some graduation ceremony, eh?" he adds lamely.

"Grandpa White fought in Korea," Sammy chimes in.

Grandpa White chuckles nervously. "Only because I had to, little man."

"Korea?" Mr. Tabata seizes on the comment. "You were fighting the Chinese, weren't you?" He glances around with an amused look. Across the table, Nai Nai's smile widens and grows brittle. Ana's eyes narrow. She flashes Jamie a look, but he's too busy being monopolized by Amanda Conrad to see it.

Grandpa White gives Mr. Tabata a friendly smile. "We were fighting the Red Army. I was fighting whoever my country told me to fight. Have you ever been a soldier, Mr. Tabata?"

Mr. Tabata clears his throat. His dark business suit gleams in the lantern light. "No, I can't say that I have."

"Then count it among your blessings," Grandpa White says. "Now, who wants to say grace?"

There is some shuffling at the table and Ana starts to say something—her mother's parents are far more Christian than Ana was raised to be. Nai Nai is a Buddhist, Chelsea's family is nonreligious and the Tabatas . . . they could be anything. Same with Amanda Conrad. But before she can think of what to say, Grandpa White nods.

"All right then, I guess it'll be me." He folds his large hands together and bows his head. Ana does the same, although she's dying to see what the rest of the group does.

"Bless this food we are about to receive. May it help our children grow strong and wise and comfort us old people too. Amen."

"Amen," Ana says, and hears it echo around the table. She smiles at Grandpa White. Chelsea whispers to Ana, "He's my favorite."

Covers come off plates and steaming food is passed around. The delicious scent of spicy gumbo and the sweet-savory aroma of the lion's head meatballs rise into the air. Ana's mouth waters and she starts to relax. It all smells amazing.

"So, Jamie, guess what? I'm off the wait list for Crossroads next year. We'll be going together!" Amanda Conrad practically wiggles in her seat like an excited Chihuahua. Ana and Chelsea roll their eyes at each other.

"Isn't that wonderful, Jamie?" Mr. Tabata exclaims in a way that makes Ana think he already knew. Mr. Tabata slides a lion's head meatball onto his plate and passes it to Jamie. For Jamie's mom, he dishes up a spoonful of rice and some of the gravy. Ana gives Jamie a questioning look.

"Diet," he mouths. Ana looks at Mrs. T. She needs a diet like a hole in the head. Ana shakes her head and shrugs.

"Yeah, Dad," Jamie replies, "that's great. Are you excited about University, Ana?"

Ana blushes with pleasure at the chance to take over the Amanda conversation. "Yeah. They've got a good music program."

"Cool."

Ana helps herself to a couple of dumplings. She chooses the misshapen ones that she made when she first started, before she got into the right rhythm. Sammy is already on his second bowl of gumbo.

"This is excellent, Mrs. Shen, Mrs. Shen, Mrs. White," Jamie's father says with some surprise. He chuckles. "I confess, I did not know what to expect when you invited us."

"Neither did we," Ana whispers to Chelsea, with a chin nod toward Amanda and her mother. Chelsea giggles and swats Ana's leg under the table.

"But this is delightful. I spent some time in the South. Your gumbo is unusual and delicious. And the lion's head—it's similar to a dish my mother used to make, with chicken instead of pork."

"I'm glad you like it, Jeffrey," Grandma White says. Ana raises an eyebrow. Leave it to Grandma White to find out Mr. Tabata's first name and use it.

Ana nudges Chelsea. "In addition to buying my love, there's also a battle going on for the best dish. Check them out."

Across the table, Nai Nai gives Grandma White a small smile. Grandma White returns with an acknowledging nod. So far, no favorites.

"Match point," Ana whispers. Chelsea chuckles.

"Ana, your dumplings turned out better than you said they would," Grandpa White says, holding up a fat pot sticker with his fork. Ana shrugs.

"Thanks. I tried." She tries to hide the shameful blush she feels prickling across her cheek.

"They're great," Jamie says, taking another from the platter. Chelsea nudges her under the table. Ana smiles, her blush deepening.

"They are very good, baby," Grandma White agrees. Ana starts to relax. Maybe, just maybe, all is forgiven between her and the grandparents. And maybe, just maybe, she's got some play with Jamie, too. She smiles across the table at him.

On cue, Amanda grabs Jamie's arm and points to his chopsticks. "Can you show me how to use those things? You make it look so easy," she drawls.

Ana deflates. "You've got to be kidding me," she whispers to Chelsea. "Like the L.A. sushi queen can't use chopsticks. Please." Chelsea makes gagging noises as Jamie self-consciously demonstrates the proper finger-as-lever technique. Ana jabs her own chopsticks into her leg. Why, oh why did she let that cow sit next to him?

"The mixed rice is unusual," Mrs. Tabata says quietly.

"Mixed rice?" Grandma White says. Nai Nai's hand shoots out across the table and grabs a spoonful of rice from the bowl. Ana cringes.

"An-nah!" Nai Nai exclaims. "You have become so hardheaded. You do not listen to a thing I say."

Ana sinks into her seat. "Sorry, Nai Nai. Sorry, Grandma." Apologizing is easier than announcing to the table that they're eating floor rice. When it comes to dinner parties, Ana doubts the three-second rule applies. "I mixed them up by mistake," she fibs in response to the questioning looks.

"Well, I like it," Jamie says. "It tastes a bit like almonds." Ana blushes again and stares at her plate.

"Thanks."

Silence descends on the table, except for the clacking of chopsticks and the clang of forks and spoons. Ana shifts in her seat. The quiet is lasting too long, even for hungry people in front of good food. It's more like people with nothing to say. Ana's stomach sinks.

"Tell the chicken story, Grandpa," Sammy pipes up. He's found a drumstick and is waving it in the air like a baton. "Chicken, chicken," he chants.

"Chicken story?" Jamie asks.

Grandpa White looks at Ana across the table. She smiles and nods. It's one of her favorites.

Grandpa White clears his throat. "Well, like we were saying earlier, I served in the war. The Korean War. About five thousand miles and a whole lifetime from this dinner table right here."

Ana relaxes a bit more. She loves her granddad's stories. He tells them in a slow, steady voice that makes you want to listen. Chelsea nudges her under the table and points her chin. Ana looks around and nods. Everyone is hanging on Grandpa White's words.

"The first thing you should know is that I am named after my father, the Reverend Derby Elias White, Senior. So when I became a corporal in the army, everybody called me Junior. That's just the way it was. . . ."

16

Well, as Corporal White, I didn't have many things to smile about. We'd been marching through the hills for two days, moving from one base camp to another, when shots rang out overhead, followed by a grenade, and the entire company found itself pinned beneath the sharp snapping missiles of a machine-gun turret. The ground exploded like popcorn, little dust devils whirling around my legs, like they were about to drag me into hell.

"Junior, move it!" my lieutenant yelled. I muscled my way toward cover, dragging my legs like any good soldier, jogging along just on my elbows and adrenaline. It was a long trip to the tree line. Not everyone made it. In fact, by the time I'd made it to cover, it was just me and Lieutenant Smith. Everyone else was out of sight, under cover, or in plain view, lying out in the road they had just left behind.

Korea. Who'd have thought I'd travel all that way around the world, just to shoot and get shot at? It was something else. In the woods, the trees had made drifts out of the pine needles. It smelled like Christmas.

"Junior, what's your real name?" Lieutenant Smith asked me.

"Derby, sir. But I don't like it."

We'd finally pulled out our weapons. I worked to clear my rifle of pine needles, clucked my tongue at the sticky sap that'd found its way onto my barrel. Nothing that would stop the firing action, but messy nonetheless.

"What about you, sir?"

"John. John Smith. Nothing to be remembered by. Not like Derby."

I grinned. "I won't be remembered by Derby, sir. It was my father's name. And he used it all up."

"Oh yeah? Famous in his own right?"

"In his circles, yeah. The first black man to preach in a white church in Tuscaloosa, Alabama."

"You don't say?"

I paused. Lieutenant Smith was white. It was the first time the army had allowed mixed platoons. Ten years before World War Two, I would have never met Lieutenant Smith. And if I had, I wouldn't have spoken first, or even looked him in the eye. Times had changed. Lying on the soft mattress of Korean pine, I tried to think up a joke about strange *bedfellows, and came up short. Then sniper fire rang out in the branches over our heads.*

"You a racist, Lieutenant Smith?"

"Are you?"

I thought about it and said, "I don't think so. I pretty much like or hate on a personal basis."

Lieutenant Smith snorted. "So you're a selective racist?"

"Race isn't the issue. It's integrity," I said definitively.

Smith smiled at me. "Now, that sounds like the son of a preacher."

I smiled back. "Amen."

That's when the enemy came through the trees. Smith stood up, shouting, and the ground fighting began.

I killed three men that day, all of them with yellow skin, desperate eyes and Russian rifles. Miraculously, Lieutenant Smith and I both survived.

"What are you thinking about?" Smith asked me as we loaded into the caravan and drove the last few miles to camp.

"Pros and cons, sir, pros and cons."

"Meaning?"

"The best thing about this war is you and me right now. Talking at our ease like we might have always done. The worst thing is, I have to kill men for the privilege."

Smith hung his head a little lower. "First kill, Junior?"

"No, sir. First friendly conversation with a white man."

Smith broke into a grin. "Ain't life a witch?"

"Not really, sir." I smiled back. "Not today."

But the day wasn't over. And the three miles to camp were longer than we could have known.

The caravan came to a halt two miles from camp. A bridge that had been there that morning was gone. The stream was shallow, but the banks were too steep for driving.

"We've got to go around the long way, sir," the driver said. "It'll take a couple of hours, or you can walk it."

A couple of hours was more than us men wanted to give. So we jumped down from the truck and forded the stream without trouble, guns over our heads, pants wet to the knees.

Lieutenant Smith told us to head west and fan out.

So I followed the others into the trees.

Not more than half a mile along, I heard voices and dropped to the ground. I could just picture my mother asking me, "Derby Elias White, what in tarnation have you gotten yourself into?"

Lying on my back against a shallow hillside, hoping the soldiers on the other side of the rise were American and not Chinese, I stretched my ears as far as they would go. Somebody was speaking, and it wasn't English.

I lay there, covered in dust the exact color of cinnamon. Funny what you remember at a time like that. "Spread out, fan out," the lieutenant had said. That's how men got lost. That's how I ended up with the Red Army marching right on top of me.

Night fell with me hugging that hillside and my stomach growling loud enough to sound the alarm.

"I have got to eat," I told myself. Eat now, march later.

So I slid off my hillside and made it to the tree line, watching my back every step of the way. Someone could be hiding behind the next bush, asleep on the bed of pine needles *in front of me, who knew? An hour had passed on my watch by the time I came across an abandoned farm.*

The gate to the cattle paddock was broken open. The chicken coop had been half burned by a fallen lantern. The shack that served as a farmhouse was empty as a shell. I took shelter in the woodpile, where I could get back to the woods quickly and have a good view of the yard.

The moon was full, and everything was deep blue and hard to see. My stomach was growling fit to wake the dead.

I was trying to keep it quiet when something moved in the farmyard. I set my service rifle at the ready. Whatever was moving was low to the ground. So I squint a little harder and see it was a chicken.

Just a regular old chicken, scratching in the yard.

So I relax a little and get to thinking, Maybe that bird laid some eggs somewhere nearby. Or better yet, maybe the farmhouse had a kitchen. I just needed a fire, some frying oil and a little flour. . . .

I was going to make me some Southern-style deep-fried chicken. Now, I had to come up with a plan first. See, if you shoot at a bird, you could miss, or worse, fill it up with bullets and bile. No, an eating bird has to be caught by hand.

So I hid my rifle in the woodpile, where I could grab it quickly if I needed to but nobody walking by would see it right away. Then I sized up the chicken scratching around in the dirt. I crouched down low, tightened the strap on my helmet and spat in both hands. Just like on my grandma's farm. Just. Like. It.

And I dove at the bird.

Only, someone else did too. I screamed, I was so surprised. The chicken shrieked and ran. I grabbed for my pistol but it wasn't there, and my rifle was too far away.

So I look up to see what I'm facing. And it's another soldier. Chinese, helmetless. Gunless. Dirty and tired. Just like me. Hungry, too. Caught diving for a chicken, just like me.

I raised my hands, but not too high, so he'd know I was backing off but not surrendering. He looked around and I did too. We were alone. Then this Chinese fellow raised his hands a little too.

"No gun," I said, but the poor man was too scared to speak.

We looked like we were praying in a country church, both of us on our knees like that in the middle of the yard. And then we hear a clucking, and lo and behold it's the chicken, come back to scratch in the dirt.

Now, the both of us sit there staring at that chicken. My stomach growled, and his did too. That was all the conversation we needed. With barely a nod, in perfect unison, we dove for that bird and caught it.

So we start cheering and clapping each other on the back. The guy lets go of the bird long enough for me to wring its neck.

"Shu," the Chinese fellow said, and pointed to the water pump across the yard. Turns out the farm had a kitchen after all. Not more than a tripod over a fire pit, and an old blackened pot, but it was enough. We spent half the night, two men without a single common word between them, boiling water to scald the chicken and pluck its feathers.

When it was done, the other guy pulled out a knife and divided the bird in two. I found a clay jar of oil, and the other fellow came up with small sack of either cornmeal or flour.

He brings them over to me by the fire and says something I can't follow. But I figure it's simple enough. So I mime a few things, and he nods and starts cutting up the chicken into pieces.

Now, I was wishing we had some salt to season the meat. And I didn't speak Chinese, but I did have a few words of Korean because we had a Korean fellow who helped us out in the kitchen sometimes back at camp.

So I turned to the guy and tried it out: "Sogum?"

This fellow stared at me for a good long time, and I'm thinking I've gone and made a mistake and offended him. Then the guy smiled and went outside. I sat there hoping he wasn't coming back with a gun or the rest of his platoon. My rifle was still outside. I was thinking about grabbing that chicken and running.

But my guy came back and this time he had a small bag with him. He pulled out an even smaller cloth bag and tossed it to me. I didn't know it then, but it was ginger. At the time, I was saying, "No, no. We need salt, sogum," but he insisted.

Then he reached back into his bag and came up with a little brown bottle.

"Jiang you," he said, and opened the bottle. He shook a couple of drops of brown liquid onto his finger and tasted it. "Jiang you." He held it out to me. It took a minute, but

137

I tasted it. It was soy sauce, and I figured it would do just fine.

With water from my own canteen, he washed out my helmet, and I made a batter with the flour. Meanwhile, the other fellow dumped soy sauce on the chicken parts and heated the oil in the pot on the fire. It took a good long while, and by the time we were done, it was sunrise, but there was a batch of almost authentic Southern fried chicken served on a straw mat in Korea that day.

The Chinese fellow seemed to like it. He nodded and ate three pieces. I must've had three or four. I remember that man wrapped the last piece carefully in a piece of cloth.

Then we put out the fire and waited until the oil had cooled. It sure would've been wrong to burn down the place that had given us shelter.

When the oil was cool, we went outside. I washed my helmet at the water pump and slung it on again, still wet, but safer than going without one.

We stood in the yard for a minute and I thought about shaking hands with him, but it didn't seem right. We might've been killing each other come tomorrow.

Well, he must've agreed, because he waved to me quickly and walked back into the trees. I watched him for a moment, then went in the opposite direction, toward the woodpile. I picked up my rifle and walked back toward camp. It was a long walk, but the chicken helped. It certainly did.

17

Ana feels like giving her grandfather a kiss. Everyone nods appreciatively after the story, and if they didn't have a piece of chicken before, they all have one now.

"This is delicious," Mrs. Conrad says to Ana's mom.

"Thank you." Ana's mom nods. "Would you like to try the lion's head? It's a family favorite." She holds up the dish.

"Oh . . . I don't eat tofu," Mrs. Conrad whispers. She flashes a coy look across the table to Chelsea's dad. He clears his throat and wipes his mouth of fried chicken crumbs.

"I know what you mean. My ex-wife was a vegetarian. I think that's one of the reasons we split up."

"Gross," Chelsea whispers to Ana. "They're flirting."

"No, they're not," Ana replies.

"Well, there is no tofu in this," Ana's mom says. "Just ground pork and vegetables. But I'll be glad to bring you something else. We've got the second course coming out soon." Ana smiles. Her mother's explanation is so smooth you'd never guess that the dinner almost got canceled.

Mrs. Conrad blushes. "Oh no, it's delicious. I'm fine. Thank you." She smiles nervously, then looks at Chelsea's dad and tosses her hair.

"See?" Chelsea insists.

Ana winces. "Amanda Conrad's so gonna be your new sister."

"This is your fault."

Ana shrugs innocently.

"So, Ana, tell everyone about your graduation present," Nai Nai calls from across the table.

A cold spike of adrenaline shoots through Ana's body. "Oh, right." Under the table, Chelsea digs a hand into her thigh. "Ow! Um . . . I mean, yeah, I'm really lucky. My grandparents are taking me on two trips. Uh, Nai Nai and Ye Ye are taking me to Taiwan, and Grandma and Grandpa White found this great cruise thing. Down the Mississippi. With music. It's a music cruise. It's gonna be great."

The Tabatas and Chelsea's family look at her a little oddly. Ana's smile is plastered onto her face so wide her cheeks hurt. She avoids looking at her parents. Nai Nai breaks into a proud smile. "Ana hasn't been to Taiwan since she was a baby. So really it will be her first time."

"Sounds awesome," Jamie says.

"Yeah, awesome," Chelsea chimes in.

Amanda Conrad giggles and whispers something in Jamie's ear. Ana glares at her, but Nai Nai is talking again.

"Ana is a very lucky girl, very smart. We are so proud of her."

"Yes, very proud," Grandma White says suddenly. Ana blushes. She looks to her mom for help. Her mother clears her throat.

"I'm sure we're all proud of our graduates," she says equitably.

"Yes, the children have acquitted themselves quite well today," Mr. Tabata says. Jamie squirms under his father's heavy-handed back patting.

"Education is so important," Grandma White adds. "Derby and I are going to make sure Ana has every opportunity in life. And Sammy, too."

Ana starts to cringe. It can only get worse from here.

On cue, Nai Nai steps up to the plate. "Yuan and I are going to give her a house one day."

"Really?" Mr. Tabata's eyes widen.

"Real estate!" Mrs. Conrad exclaims. "What a good idea!" She pats Ana's mom on the shoulder admiringly.

"It's very Asian, actually," Mr. Tabata says. "To provide for your children in such a way. It ensures that they can provide for you when they are older."

Ana wants to crawl under the table. "No way am I taking care of Nai Nai," she whispers to Chelsea.

Chelsea giggles. "Maybe you can take care of Chuck," she whispers back. Ana elbows her in the ribs.

Grandma White and Nai Nai are giving each other looks across the table, but they don't say anything. Apparently having dinner guests really does keep the peace. Ana tries to act nonchalant as she serves herself another scoop of rice.

Mr. Tabata chuckles. "It's admirable that you are trying to raise your daughter as both Chinese and black."

"I *am* Chinese and black," Ana says. Her parents give Mr. Tabata a questioning look.

Mr. Tabata picks up his soup spoon. "Yes, yes, of course. James, why don't you tell them what we gave you today?"

Jamie gives Ana an apologetic look that instantly makes her feel warm inside.

"Oh, Jamie, what did you get?" Amanda looks like she'll explode if she doesn't find out. Ana rolls her eyes. Jamie sinks down a little in his seat.

"Um . . . a car."

"What?" Ana says.

"No way!" Chelsea exclaims.

Amanda looks like she's going to pass out.

"See, Dad?" Ana says.

"But . . . you're too young to drive," Ana's father tells her.

"I'm too young to own a house, too."

Jamie clears his throat. "Well, I'll be old enough for a permit this winter, and I can take driver's ed next year. Until then, my mom can use it." He looks embarrassed. "It's nothing fancy. But it's nice."

"Well, great," Ana says. "Maybe you can show it to us sometime."

Jamie smiles at her and Ana remembers why she's here in the first place. "Yeah, that'd be cool."

"I wish I had a car," Amanda says with a look at her mother. Her mom grins awkwardly.

"You do, honey. It's *our* car."

"Yeah, right." Amanda folds her arms and pouts. Ana gives Chelsea a look.

"A car is a big responsibility for a child," Ana's mother says to Mrs. Tabata.

"I believe in teaching children responsibility while they're young," Mr. Tabata responds for his wife. "That is what makes them excel. It's why James is the head of his class today. If you encourage second-rate, you get second-rate. I encourage the best."

Ana's heart pounds a little harder. Her mother's eyes narrow. So do Grandma White's.

"As do we, Mr. Tabata," her mother says. She glances at Ana as if to say, "Are you sure this boy is worth the trouble?" Ana shrugs back.

"Well, first or second, I think they're both pretty wonderful," Grandpa White says. "Just like the second course is going to be just as good as the first. Helen, what have we got coming next?"

Ana's mom rises a little too quickly. "Daniel, weren't you going to stir-fry the *mapo*?"

Ana's dad stands up. "Right away. Right away." He disappears into the kitchen.

Chelsea's dad says something that makes Mrs. Conrad laugh. Dina and Sammy are making faces at each other across the table.

"Hey, want to see our garden?" Ana asks Jamie. It's like taking recess halfway through a test. Everyone gets up, moves around the backyard, breathes a little. Amanda Conrad tries to follow them, but Chelsea hangs back in the gateway to the side yard and blocks her.

"I want to see the garden too," Amanda says.

"What garden?" Chelsea winks at Ana when Jamie's back is turned.

"Sorry about my dad," Jamie says once they are in the side yard staring at the tangle of mint and sage. "He can be kind of abrupt sometimes."

"No, no problem," Ana says. "My family's no picnic either. They're driving me crazy."

Jamie laughs. "Yeah. Too bad they had to cancel the dance. At least then all we'd have to deal with would be teachers."

"No kidding," Ana says.

Her heartbeat is getting louder in her ears. Suddenly, she wishes she had changed into that sundress.

"Sorry we didn't get to hear your speech." Jamie takes a step toward her, his hands clasped behind his back. Ana feels her face grow warm.

"Round two, everyone!" Grandpa White hollers out across the backyard. Ana straightens up. Right. Romance in a garden full of parents. A spicy scent drifts in over the bright smell of the mint. She clears her throat.

"Sounds like the *mapo*'s done. You should have some. It's really good."

They all move back to the table with its new steaming dishes. Ana reluctantly takes her seat a whole table-width away from Jamie.

"This is delicious!" Mrs. Conrad exclaims, shoveling in a forkful of *mapo dofu* dripping with saucy ground pork tinged red by pepper and oil.

"Yeah, it's great," Chelsea's dad says with his mouth full. "What's it called again?"

"Mapo," Ana's mom says. *"Mapo dofu.* It essentially means . . . stir-fried tofu."

Chelsea's dad and Mrs. Conrad both pause in mid-chew. "Really?" Mrs. Conrad says slowly. Chelsea leans against Ana and breaks into giggles. Ana joins her. But neither of the adults stops eating.

"Leave room for dessert," Grandma White says. "We've got cake and ice cream."

Choruses of enthusiasm rise around the table. "Yay!" Sammy shouts. "Cake and ice cream!"

Mr. Tabata chuckles. Ana can feel her hair stand on end. She tries to ignore it.

"Such a wonderful fusion of cuisines tonight," he says. Not "Wow, this is good," but "fusion of cuisines."

"Who talks like that?" Chelsea whispers. Ana and Jamie exchange a look across the table.

"This is soooo good," Amanda purrs. "Try it, Jamie." Ana can practically feel the steam coming out of her ears as Amanda offers him a bite of tofu, suddenly skillful with her chopsticks.

Mr. Tabata leans across Jamie and taps Amanda's arm.

"If I didn't know better, Amanda, I'd say you have your sights set on my son." Amanda blushes and tosses her hair in a honey-colored cloud that Ana's sure will send strands flying into everyone's food.

"Oh, Mr. Tabata, don't tease me," Amanda says. It's so practiced, such a perfect sidestep from what should have been a total embarrassment meltdown, that it makes Ana sick. Her mouth fills with a sourness no amount of gumbo or lemonade can erase.

Jamie looks at Ana again, but she looks away before they can make eye contact. She wants to die.

"God, are they gonna get engaged right here?" Chelsea whispers.

"Mrs. Conrad, your daughter is a delight," Mr. Tabata calls down the table.

Mrs. Conrad smiles. "Mandy was voted most popular in her class."

"Most popular hag," Chelsea whispers. Ana snorts.

Mr. Tabata beams at Amanda and her mom. "I bet you've never eaten like this before, Amanda. Such a wonderfully multicultural meal." He chuckles and Ana's stomach tightens into a knot. There's that phrase again, the one her social sciences teacher used to use. Mr. Tabata spreads his hands delightedly. "It's like . . ." He searches for the words. ". . . like a food court at the mall."

Ana's face grows hot. She puts down her napkin. Pushes away from the table. Stands up.

And throws a dumpling at Mr. Tabata.

"Honey!" her mom says.

"Young lady!" Mr. Tabata roars.

Chelsea laughs. "That was awesome."

Jamie's eyes go huge and he stifles a snort. Sammy starts chanting, "Food fight, food fight," but Ana's dad grabs his arms before he can throw anything.

"Don't waste good food," Nai Nai cries, chopsticks in midair, as if she could somehow catch the thrown dumpling.

"Ana, what are you doing?" her dad asks through gritted teeth.

"Sorry, Dad. I'm just trying to get Mr. Tabata's attention. And now that I have it . . ." She takes a deep breath. "You have got to be the rudest person I've ever met. I mean, we invite you to dinner, and you call it a food court? This isn't a food court. This is my house! And it's clear you're horrified that your son might actually like me. I mean, I may not be a hundred percent Chinese or black or a hundred percent anything, and God knows I'm not a blonde, but this is still my family, and my dinner and my house. And you can respect us or you can leave."

"Ana!" her dad exclaims.

"This is lunacy," Mr. Tabata roars.

"Ana, apologize," her mother says in a tired voice.

"What? For real?" Ana stares at her parents in shock.

Ana's mother hesitates. "This is not the way to make friends," she explains steadily. And, in that sentence, Ana can see it: all the years her mother has held her tongue against the judgments of family and strangers, too. All the times her father has kept quiet or joked and pretended it didn't matter what people thought of his black wife and half-breed kids.

All the times Grandma White has had to listen to jokes about marrying a black man named White. Every barb and insult Grandpa White endured in a newly desegregated army while serving his country at war. And all the doors shut in Nai Nai's face when they first came to the United States, trying to rent an apartment or buy groceries with the wrong accent and the wrong skin.

It makes Ana shake.

It makes her want to scream.

Instead, she picks up another lumpy dumpling, looks at Mr. Tabata, and says, "Leave."

18

"She's right," Ana's mother says. Ana's dad stands up from the table. Even Sammy is quiet, eyes wide. The Shens and the Whites all look deathly serious. Mr. Tabata's mouth shrinks into a thin line.

"Come on, Jamie. I will not be insulted in front of my family." Mr. Tabata gets up from the table, wiping his mouth as if to wipe away a bad taste. Jamie's mother hesitates, then slowly rises.

"The meal was delicious," she says apologetically. Mr. Tabata glares at her.

"Jamie."

Jamie doesn't move. He stares straight ahead at Ana

and there are tears in his eyes, building slowly from a shine to a clouded veil, trembling at each word as he begins to speak. Ana knows Jamie's not looking at her. He's just *not* looking at his dad really hard.

"No, Dad. I'm staying."

"Jamie! These people aren't worth your time."

Jamie turns on his father, a tear spilling over.

" 'These people' are my friends, Dad. I've known Ana for nine years, ever since kindergarten. She's been in every play and assembly with me since we were five years old. Have you ever even noticed her? Or anybody else? Of course not."

Jamie looks across the table at Ana. "I'm sorry, Ana. I'm sorry I let him put you guys through this." Ana blushes but can't think of a response.

Jamie turns to his mother and puts a hand on her shoulder. "And you, Mom . . . I'm sorry I didn't say something sooner."

Jamie's mom turns red. Jamie clears his throat and looks up at his father.

"Dad, you bully her, and it's not right. Let her eat what she wants, let her have the car. I don't want it.

"You boss us around and I keep quiet. When you push me, I tell myself it's because you care. I work hard in school so you'll be proud of me. But it's not enough. I've tried to be a good son. Why can't you be a better father?"

Jamie's mom buries her face in her hands. After a moment, she wipes her eyes and walks away. Ana's mother follows her into the house.

Mr. Tabata just stands there, suit coat clutched in one hand like a life buoy. His mouth moves but no words come out. Ana wishes she could read his mind. Instead, she gets up and goes to stand behind Jamie. He reaches back and takes her hand.

The movement wakes Mr. Tabata out of his daze. He drapes his jacket across his arm, clears his throat and removes his glasses to polish them casually on his sleeve.

"This is a family matter," he says in a strained voice. "We will discuss it at home."

Ana squeezes Jamie's hand. Jamie is trembling, but he stands his ground. Everyone watches as Jamie's father replaces his glasses, pulls on his jacket and leaves the table in search of his wife.

19

There is a long moment of silence. Ana doesn't know what to say. Slowly, Jamie lets go of her hand and sits down. He clears his throat.

"So," he says in a strained voice, "who wants dessert?"

Amanda Conrad giggles, and her mother shushes her.

"Son, are you all right?" Grandpa White asks.

Jamie clears his throat again. "Yeah. Thanks."

Ana looks at her grandparents desperately. She wants to give Jamie a hug, or run and hide in her bedroom. Instead she just stands there. Grandma White and Nai Nai rise at the same time.

"I believe Ana's mother had a cake she was decorating," Grandma White announces.

"And I am going to make my mango pudding," Nai Nai says. They both leave the table.

"Sounds great," Grandpa White says. "I'll get some tinfoil for all this food."

"We're in for a treat," Ana's dad tells everyone. "Ma's mango pudding is legendary." He sounds so fake-cheerful it puts Ana's teeth on edge. Why did she say anything to Mr. Tabata? Her mother was right. What could be worse than this?

Ana's dad starts to clear the table for dessert and everyone drifts off to admire the herb garden, read the graduation sign and just get away from the scene of the crime. Jamie stays seated at the table, still sprinkled with rice, napkins and empty plates, like the last person at a parade. Ana shifts uncomfortably. She crouches down to face him.

"Jamie, I'm sorry."

Jamie looks at her. His eyes are a little red, but that's all. "It's fine, Ana. It had to happen someday. Sorry it happened at your party."

Ana shrugs. "That's okay. But it was my fault. I should've kept my mouth shut."

"Right," Jamie says. "You should've stopped being Ana Shen."

Ana shrugs. "That's not such a bad idea."

"You're kidding, right? I mean, you're Ana Shen. You stood up for your family, and you're smart, and you're pretty, and you're a nice person. Why would you want to be anything other than that?"

Ana takes a deep breath and pulls herself into the seat next to Jamie.

"You know, before you came over, I would have given anything to not be in this family. Sometimes we just really hate each other. My grandmother was actually mad at me when she found out I wasn't valedictorian. She called me lazy. And my other grandmother thought I 'let you win' "—she makes air quotes—"because I like you."

Jamie smirks. "Yeah, I was gonna let you be valedictorian, but my dad would've killed me."

Ana laughs. "They could start a club together."

"The pushy-pushy club," Jamie says. They both laugh.

Ana looks around the yard and sighs. "Then again, here we are, top of our class."

Jamie looks at his hands. "High school's gonna suck."

"Yeah." Ana pats his knee and folds her hands into her lap. "Families kind of stink."

Jamie laughs. "Yours is pretty cool."

Ana frowns. "I didn't think so, until now."

Jamie sighs. "Well, I wish I had a better one."

He looks at Ana and she passes him a paper napkin to wipe his eyes. "Who knows?" she says. "Now that it's all out in the open, maybe you will."

Jamie shrugs and sighs. "Maybe."

The evening settles around them softly, the day's heat rising in waves from the ground into the air.

"So," Jamie says after a moment. "You like me."

Ana reddens. She clears her throat. "According to my grandmother."

That garners a small smile.

Ana bites her lip. "And you think I'm pretty."

Jamie blushes. "Very."

Ana smiles wryly and nods. "Cool."

20

In the kitchen, Nai Nai shakes her head. *What a scene tonight,* she thinks. *What a scene.* No matter the differences in their family, she would never have made it so public, so obvious and embarrassing. She hears the front door slam as Mr. Tabata goes home alone. *Good riddance to him.* She relaxes her shoulders.

Lighten up, Mei, she tells herself. Today should be a day for celebration. Nai Nai smiles. Here she is, cooking mango pudding in her son's kitchen, his troublesome wife right behind her, icing Ana's graduation cake. That Japanese boy's mother is sitting at the table, watching. She stopped crying a few minutes ago, after telling her husband to go home. That's good. *Take time to calm down,* Nai Nai thinks. *Besides, no one is worth your tears.*

She steals a glance over her shoulder. Whatever she might think of Ana's mother, the woman has a talented eye. A jungle of brightly colored icings has sprung up in bowls alongside the giant sheet cake. Nai Nai had worried it would be served plain as a coffee cake, inappropriate for her granddaughter's big day.

She shrugs and turns back to her pudding. Her daughter-in-law is an artist. Let her do her art. The pot is almost at a boil now. *Too hot, too fast,* Nai Nai chides herself, and lowers the flame. The air is heavy with ripe mango. Nai Nai's mouth waters. Too hot and too fast. She was like that once too.

"Mei, he's too old for you!"

"He is not," Mei said for the umpteenth time. Teacher Shen was handsome, refined, even mature, but not old. "Besides, he said he liked the flowers I brought him yesterday."

"It's just creepy, Mei," her best friend, Ton Li, said with a shiver. "And he's not even a real teacher. He's a substitute! You're seventeen. You can do better than a substitute teacher."

The two girls were smoking filterless cigarettes smuggled in from the Ukraine, blowing the smoke out the window of the third-floor girls' bathroom in the Taipei School for Charming Young Women, or the Harm School, as the girls called it. It was a reform school, no matter what the shingle said on the outside. Even the principal knew that his students smoked in the bathroom. The ashtrays with the school logo on them were evidence of that. Mei and Ton Li puffed streams of smoke out the window as the only act of defiance left them—showing their bad behavior to the whole world.

"Besides, also," Mei declared, "Lee Yuan is better than some greasy-faced punk from Gordon's." Gordon's was the British-run brother school of the Harm.

"True, true," Ton Li conceded. The girls finished their cigarettes just as the lunch bell rang. They squirted their mouths with violet perfume, checked each other's hair and headed to the cafeteria. Skipping out on English lessons was one thing, but lunch was the social event of the school. Gossip, fashion and school politics held sway at the girls' table. Besides which, Teacher Shen would be there.

"Ah, Mei," Shen Yuan said when Mei made sure to brush up against him in the food line. "Eating like a bird again, I see."

"I have no appetite," Mei said as melodramatically as she could.

Teacher Shen frowned. He was a handsome man, Mei thought, and she tilted her head down to appear shy.

"Is something amiss?" he asked. "Perhaps you should see the school nurse." He put down his tray and patted his pockets for a permission slip.

"Oh, no, no, not that," Mei said. Normally, she would jump at a free hall pass, but that wasn't her goal today. "What I have, no nurse can cure."

"Really? Bitten by a tsetse fly?" the teacher asked, chuckling.

"Some other sort of bug," Mei said coyly. "A love bug." She batted her eyelashes at him and sauntered away in her best imitation of the American movie star Marilyn Monroe. Ton Li watched all this from their usual table, monitoring her friend's success.

"Well?" Mei asked breathlessly as she sat down.

"Well, first of all, you forgot your lunch tray. And secondly, I don't think he noticed the walk. Or you didn't do it right."

"Aie. No. Should I do it again?"

"What, and look desperate?"

"Well, you're no help." Mei pouted. "And I'm hungry, too."

Her lunch tray appeared in front of her, with an extra helping of rice and sweet mango pudding.

"Good, your appetite is returning, Miss Choi. A quick recovery is a sign of good blood." Teacher Shen stood over them. He handed Mei a napkin and turned to Ton Li.

"See you in mathematics, Miss Ho."

"Bon appétit, Teacher Shen," Ton Li sang as he walked away.

"Ugh. So embarrassing," Mei said. She ate all her pudding anyway.

Two weeks later, Teacher Shen left for a job at an American university in California. Mei had been cutting class when the announcement was made, so she missed out on her opportunity for a melodramatic farewell.

A year after that, when Mei was on the verge of her nineteenth birthday, Shen Yuan came home for a holiday. She found him in her parents' sitting room, an American-made hat on his knee. Apparently, she had done the walk just right. Better than any of the American girls he'd met since then.

With her parents' permission (not an easy thing, as her father was a staunch military man, seven kills in the air force against the Japanese), they courted for the week, during which he convinced Mei to take night classes. Her grades were much higher without the distraction of Teacher Shen around, and she was accepted into the business program at the University of California, Los Angeles, for the following September. The wedding was in July. Before the first semester was over, a baby was on the way. Of course, continuing with classes was out of the question.

Nai Nai sings to herself, watching the sugar dissolve into the evaporated milk and softened agar-agar. Bitter and sweet. Like leaving Taiwan. Nai Nai smiles. She cannot wait to introduce Ana to her best friend, Ton Li. Second in her class. Imagine it.

She adds the cubes of ripened mango, popping one in her mouth. Her first kiss had been with Yuan the night before their wedding. He had tasted of mangoes. That night, she had asked her mother to show her how to make this pudding—so simple, but it made her new husband so happy. A taste of home, he would say whenever she found time to make it.

• • •

"Nai Nai. Nai Nai!" Ana waves her hand in front of Nai Nai's face.

"*Aie!* What are you doing, assaulting me like that?" Nai Nai exclaims with a start.

"I've been calling your name forever. Do you want a cup of tea?" Ana raises her eyebrows. The day's been weird enough without Nai Nai going senile on her.

"Well, I did not hear you. No, I do not want tea. Not now. Can't you see I'm thinking?"

"About what?"

Nai Nai taps the spoon on the edge of the pot and points it warningly at Ana. "None of your business, Miss Nosy-pants. Go help your mother."

Ana sighs. "Okay, fine." She turns and looks at her mother, who is decorating the sheet cake. Ana's mom shrugs.

"I'm making tea for Jamie and his mom," Ana announces, filling a kettle. "They're in the living room. Talking."

Ana drops into a chair at the table and waits for the water to boil. She rests her head on her arms and watches as bright blue flowers and butterflies emerge from her mother's bag of icing.

"You okay, honey?" her mom asks.

Ana nods, her eyes losing focus. "What a weird day."

The kitchen door opens.

"Mei, sweet, sweet Mei," Ye Ye calls in Mandarin, coming into the kitchen. Ana's eyes go wide.

161

"What?" her mother whispers. "What did he say?"

"He called her sweet," Ana says incredulously.

Ye Ye puts his arms around Nai Nai's waist.

"Did everything get put away?" Nai Nai asks.

Ye Ye shrugs. "Are you making extra pudding for me?"

Nai Nai shrugs. "Perhaps. For someone who deserves it."

Ye Ye kisses Nai Nai on the cheek. "We all deserve it," he says.

At the table, leaning over the cake, Ana and her mom try to hide their surprise, concentrating on the icing blooming into flowers around the corners. Ana shakes her head.

"See, weird day."

Ana's mom stifles a chuckle. "It's not *so* strange. I mean, they did make your dad."

"Gross, Mom."

On the stove, the kettle starts to whistle. "You sure nobody wants any?" Ana asks, pouring water into a mug. Tea seems like an inadequate offering to the Tabatas, but it's all Ana has.

"We're sure," her mom says.

Ana's mom picks up a second pastry bag, fat with red icing. With steady pressure from her right hand, guiding with her left, she writes between the flowers and curling borders in careful cursive, HAPPY GRADUATION DAY, ANA, CHELSEA AND JAMIE. After a moment's thought, she adds a blue butterfly next to Jamie's name. Ana sees it and smiles.

"Thank you." Ana's dad is suddenly standing behind her. Ana almost drops the second mug.

"Yikes, didn't see you there."

Ana's dad smiles. His arms are full of Tupperware.

"Just packing food away."

"Thank you for what?" she asks.

He shrugs. "Thank you for standing up for us out there. That was brave and well aimed, if a little awkward."

He smiles, empties his armload onto the counter and kisses Ana on the cheek. Turning to Ana's mom, he takes a swipe from a bowl of red icing and eats it absently.

"Look at those two." He points with his chin at his parents, dancing to the tune of his mother's humming. "It's disgusting."

Ana's mom giggles and wipes the icing off her hands with her apron. "Simply vile," she says, and leans in to Ana's dad for a sugary kiss.

"For crying out loud, people." Ana grabs her tea mugs and flees.

21

"Good night," Ana says. Jamie and his mother were the first to leave, in a cab half an hour earlier. Now Ana leans against the doorjamb and waves as Chelsea and her family leave with Amanda Conrad and her mother in tow.

Amanda hangs up her cell phone. "Mom, can you drop me off at the movies? I can still catch up with those other guys." She tucks her arm into her mom's elbow.

"Let's just see, honey," her mother says, and hurries to catch up with Chelsea's dad.

Chelsea's dad's arms are laden with leftovers, and everyone looks kind of worn out. The sky has gone a deep purply blue and the stars are hanging overhead. The air feels like a warm bath. Ana is tired to her very bones.

Chelsea hangs back as the others go around the corner of the hedge. "Yo, Shen," she hisses. "This is your fault!"

Ana smiles and shrugs. "Blame Cupid," she whispers back. Chelsea gives a mock frown, then holds her hand up like a phone.

"Call me," she mouths. Ana does the same and nods.

Back inside, her dad is giving Sammy a bath upstairs. Ana can hear Sammy splashing around. She walks down the hallway and sees Grandpa White taking off his glasses and sitting on the edge of the guest bed.

"Good night, Grandpa."

"Good night, honey. Thanks for the unusual evening."

Ana laughs. "Any time."

In the living room, Ye Ye is watching an action film on TV. "Good night, Ye Ye."

"Hmm? Oh, good night, Ana. Good night."

Ana smiles to herself and walks back to the kitchen, where her grandmothers are packing up the last of the cake and pudding.

"Thank you, Nai Nai. Thank you, Grandma. It was really good."

Ana's grandmothers smile at her. "You're welcome, baby girl," Grandma White says.

"Yes, Ana. It was our pleasure," Nai Nai adds. Ana gives them a group hug. Maybe Jamie was right about them.

She grabs a leftover slice of watermelon and steps out into the backyard. A breeze has finally risen from the ocean and Ana can smell seaweed and brine in the cooling

165

air. Her mom is on a stepladder, taking down the graduation banner.

"There she is," her mom says. "So, honey, you've graduated and had your first dinner date. What do you think?"

Ana laughs. "Like you have to ask."

"So, no love connection?" her mom asks.

"More like a therapy session." Ana pulls a chair over and helps take down the other side of the banner. "But it was good. I had fun."

Her mother looks over her shoulder at Ana and smiles. "Yeah, that's what first dates are like."

"I don't think it counts as a date if your entire family is there," Ana points out.

Ana's mom shrugs and climbs down from the ladder. "It counts as much as you want it to."

They fold the banner into a sloppy version of a square and Ana's mother puts it in a box in the garage. "Well, what are you going to do now?"

Ana shrugs. "Go to bed, I guess. I'm kind of tired."

Ana's mom stifles a yawn. "Yeah, you're not the only one." She pulls Ana into a hug and kisses her on the forehead. "Congratulations, honey. I'm very proud of you."

"Yeah, Mom," Ana says, embarrassed.

Her mom's smile fades. "No, Ana. I'm really very proud."

Ana looks into her mother's eyes and nods. "Yeah. Me too."

• • •

Upstairs in her bedroom, Ana opens the window to the evening breeze. The light wind ripples her pajama top and feels good along her skin. *So much for my big day,* she thinks. She looks at the clock. It's not even nine-thirty. Sad. She stands in the window a little longer.

Jamie and his mom seemed okay when they left. Like they'd handle things together somehow. *I wonder what's going on at their house right now.* Down the block, a dog starts to bark. Ana rests her head on her arm against the windowsill. She wonders if Jamie will get to keep his car. But that's the least of his problems.

Ana breathes in the night air. This was not the day she expected it to be. Not. At. All. But still, it was pretty interesting.

She lowers the window halfway and crawls into her bed. In the light from the window, her skin is a pale shade of moonlight, her hair Midnight Blue™. She yawns and tucks her head against her pillow.

I still haven't kissed a boy, she thinks. *But Jamie Tabata likes me . . . and high school doesn't start for another seventy-four days.*